Anonymo

Annual Report of the Grant Medical College, Bombay

Twelfth Year - Session 1857-58

SALZWASSER
VERLAG

Anonymous

Annual Report of the Grant Medical College, Bombay

Twelfth Year - Session 1857-58

Reprint of the original, first published in 1859.

1st Edition 2022 | ISBN: 978-3-37513-106-7

Verlag (Publisher): Salzwasser Verlag GmbH, Zeilweg 44, 60439 Frankfurt, Deutschland
Vertretungsberechtigt (Authorized to represent): E. Roepke, Zeilweg 44, 60439 Frankfurt, Deutschland
Druck (Print): Books on Demand GmbH, In de Tarpen 42, 22848 Norderstedt, Deutschland

ANNUAL REPORT

OF THE

GRANT MEDICAL COLLEGE,

BOMBAY.

TWELFTH YEAR.—SESSION 1857-58.

—————

Bombay:

PRINTED AT THE EDUCATION SOCIETY'S PRESS.

———

1858.

CONTENTS.

GRANT MEDICAL COLLEGE,

BOMBAY.

TWELFTH YEAR.—SESSION 1857-58.

.

PROFESSORS.

Principal, and Professor of Medicine..........................	C. MOREHEAD, M.D., Act. Supt. Surgeon, Poona.
Acting Principal, and Professor of Chemistry and Botany......	H. GIRAUD, M.D.
Professor of Materia Medica ...	R. HAINES, M.B.
Acting Professor of Materia Medica	G. M. C. BIRDWOOD.
Professor of Surgery	G. R. BALLINGALL, M.D.
Professor of Medical Jurisprudence	W. CAMPBELL, M.D.
Acting Professor of Ophthalmic Surgery	H. J. CARTER, Esq.
Professor of Midwifery	C. C. MEAD, Esq.
Professor of Anatomy and Physiology, Curator of the Museum, and Acting Professor of Medicine	T. M. LOWNDS, M.D.

2

ANNUAL REPORT.

THE Twelfth Session of the College was opened on the
15th June 1857. The intro-
Opening of the Session. ductory address on this occasion
was delivered by Dr. Ballingall, the Professor of Surgery.

2. Early in the month of June, Dr. Morehead having
been appointed Officiating Su-
Changes in the Professors. perintending Surgeon of the
Poona Division of the Army, the duties of Principal devolv-
ed upon myself; and those of Professor of Medicine and
Clinical Medicine upon Dr. Lownds, whose offices, of Professor of Anatomy and Physiology, and Curator of the
Museum, were entrusted to the care of Dr. Birdwood. · On
the death of the late Mr. Seaward, Mr. Haines was
re-appointed to the Chair of Materia Medica, the duties
of which he had performed with such distinguished ability
previous to its *ex-officio* connexion with the office of
Medical Storekeeper. Early in October Dr. Morehead
returned to the College, and Dr. Lownds resumed his
chair of Anatomy and Physiology and the Curatorship of
the Museum. Consequent on Mr. Haines's appointment
to the Presidency Educational Inspectorship, Dr. Birdwood was appointed, early in November, to officiate as
Professor of Materia Medica. Towards the end of

February Dr. Morehead again left us for the Poona Superintending Surgeoncy; and the same arrangements were made for the performance of his duties here as on the former occasion, at the commencement of the Session.

3. Although Dr. Morehead's official connexion with *Dr. Morehead's retirement from the College.* the College has not absolutely ceased, yet we cannot hide from ourselves the extreme improbability of his ever again presiding within these walls. And when it is remembered that to his exertions, under the approving eye of the enlightened Statesman whose name it bears, this College owes its very existence,—that under his wise and cautious, and yet liberal and practical management it has grown into so complete an Institution that it may well challenge comparison with the Medical Schools of Europe, it will be seen that his removal to another sphere of duty is an event which could not be lightly passed over in silence ; specially by one who counts it amongst the greatest privileges of his life to have been for so many years associated with him, and who, in common with every Professor and every Student, has found his sagacious, kind, and willing counsel, and his bright and active example, a sure and safe guide in difficulty, and an ever-present stimulus to exertion. But any expressions here recorded of the veneration and esteem in which we have held our Principal, are utterly inadequate to represent the depth of our grateful feelings.

4. Seventeen candidates presented themselves for matriculation. Of these, six: viz. *Admission of Students.* four Parsees, one Hindoo, and one Portuguese, were found qualified ; five of these joined the College.

5. This fact, of only six out of seventeen Candidates being found qualified, points *Defective preparatory Education of Students.* to the continuance of the defective preparatory education so emphatically dwelt upon by Dr. Morehead in the Report of last year, against which this College has had to contend for some years past; and which (as will appear from the Report of the Government Examiner) has this year, for the first time, resulted in the complete withholding of the Diploma. This is indeed a discouraging result at this advanced period in the history of the College; and it might well suggest misgivings of the future success of Medical Education here; and induce faint-heartedness on the part of those of us who, thirteen years ago, initiated, with such sanguine expectations, the working of this Institution, and who have had the pleasure and reward of witnessing the superior attainments by which, in former years, the Diploma has been won, and the confirmation that has since been given it by the public estimation of the professional skill and ability of our early Graduates. The contrast between the Graduation List of former years and the unhappy result which we now deplore, although at first sight so discouraging, is, on closer investigation, a ground for hopefulness. It proves that the Native mind is not incapable of that high cultivation required for the right discharge of professional duties, and that the cause of this falling off is but of a temporary and transient nature; and it suggests the belief that, if our now unsuccessful candidates had been conducted through that admirable early mental discipline and training, which their predecessors enjoyed at the hands of men so accomplished in the art of teaching as Harkness, Bell, Henderson, and Green,

our labours this session would, in all probability, have been crowned with a success equal at least to that of former years.

6. There was a recent period, when those who presided over the educational operations of this Presidency entertained the belief that the time had arrived when all school teaching and training might be safely entrusted to Native agency. And accordingly Native Masters, ill-acquainted with the use, and ignorant of the genius of the English language, and, above all, unskilled in the subtle and profound art of practical education, were installed in all our Schools. The experiment was intended to have a fair trial. But many, who had made education their study, were sceptical of successful results: and no wonder; for they perceived, on the one hand, the defective qualifications of the Native Masters as a class; and, on the other, the rare abilities and qualifications required of those who would successfully direct the dawning efforts of the mind. This College now testifies to the lamentable failure of the experiment. The school boys of a few years ago are now the Candidates for our Diplomas: and here, more than elsewhere perhaps, the error becomes most prominently striking, from the fact that, in the study and practice of the Medical Art, just those very qualities of mind are demanded, the implanting and cultivation of which in early years have been neglected and unheeded. The keen, penetrating, and ever-open eye of observation;—the truthful interpretation of phenomena;—the severely logical process of induction; the careful tracing of analogy;—the practical art of deduction, are all equally and absolutely necessary agencies, by which alone the Physician can detect and unravel the obscure and complex conditions of disease, and devise remedial measures.

It is in the proper exercise of these mental processes that we find our Students so sadly deficient. Memory, cultivated at school, to the neglect of the reasoning faculties, has left the healthy and independent and self-relying activity of the mind so to languish, that the College Professor finds it in vain to attempt to arouse it. I have, however, confident hope that we are now passing through our severest ordeal; and that, by an improved system of School Education; and through the exercise of the more scrupulously careful Entrance Examination, which has of late been conducted; and by enforcing the rule, which compels Students, who evince want of ability and inaptitude for learning, to withdraw from the College; and through the influence of the revised stipendiary system, lately sanctioned by Government, a more intelligent body of Students, capable of fully benefiting by the great practical advantages of this Medical School, will, for the future, annually yield a goodly number of highly qualified Practitioners. Of this, at least, I am certain, that in the course pursued by the Government Examiner and Assessors, the maxim that " honesty is the best policy" will be fully realized;—that, as it is only honest to the public and to our former Graduates to maintain the value, and not to lower the standard of our Diploma; so it will be found that this strict integrity is for the real credit of the College and the ultimate success of Medical Education here.

7. Already the Examinations for Scholarships just concluded have elicited the *Encouraging Result of the Scholarship Examinations.* gratifying fact that we have within the College a larger number of Students, who have attained to higher degrees of proficiency in the several subjects of study this year

than their predecessors have done for several preceding years. The tabular statements in the Appendix to this Report, showing the numbers gained in the Scholarship Examinations, prove this.

8. If the schools of this Presidency are capable of

Professional Prospects of the Students of this College.

supplying more highly qualified young men than those who present themselves at our Matriculation Examinations, it is difficult to perceive why they do not come to us; for, at present, no course of education holds out the prospect of such ample pecuniary emoluments, and so certain a provision for life, as the curriculum of this College. Not only does the generosity of Government here offer a professional education gratis ; but private liberality has so richly endowed us with scholarships, that a student of very ordinary ability may be supported through the whole period of his College life ; at the end of which the fostering hand of Government is again put forth to sustain him in those early years of practice, which to men of all professions in Europe are years of such arduous toil and struggle for reputation, for position, and even for daily bread. But here our Graduates may at once be enlisted in Government employ, as Sub-Assistant Surgeons, on the pay of Rs. 100 per mensem, with the prospect of advancement. How very few Graduates in England can, on leaving their "Alma Mater," at once expect to earn a hundred a year; and still further, to render the comparison just, it must be borne in mind how vast is the disproportion in value between a hundred a year to the native and to the European. But, moreover, the experience of seven years has shown us that private practice offers to our Graduates such abundant remuneration, that out of twenty-eight who have been in Government employ, as Sub-Assistant Surgeons, only eleven have found it worth their while to remain as such. But not only is there still a demand for our Graduates, as private practitioners in Bombay itself, but the great cities of Poona, Surat, Baroda, and Ahmedabad are as yet unprovided with them. Still this certain and ample provision, and this honourable position in life fail at present to induce any considerable number of properly qualified young men to exert themselves to go through the present sacrifice of five years of earnest professional study for so worthy a future reward.

9. Forty-one Students, twenty-one Student Apprentices, and five Hospital Assistants,—a total of sixty-seven

Attendance of Students.

pupils,—were in attendance on the classes at the commencement of the Session. In the course of the Session, one Student has been dismissed for dishonesty; and at the close of the examination three were required to withdraw on account of want of ability (in accordance with the 11th Article of the College Regulations). In the month of November, the requirements of the Public Service necessitated the removal from the College of all the Student Apprentices and Hospital Assistants.

10. The Reports, which I have received from the Professors of the College, en-

Course of Instruction.

able me to state that the several courses of instruction have been complete, and conducted in accordance with the Prospectus published before the commencement of the Session, with the single exception of that in Materia Medica, which, owing to the sickness and death of the late Mr. Seaward, was not commenced till the end of August.

11. At the close of the Session eighteen Candidates for " First Examination Certificates" presented themselves. Of these, thirteen were found qualified.

First Certificate Examination.

12. The " Final Examination" was conducted by Dr. Arbuckle, Civil Surgeon, as Government Examiner ;

Diploma Examination.

Dr. Winchester, Medical Storekeeper ; Mr. Glasse, Surgeon to the 2nd Battalion Artillery ; Mr. Woosnam, Surgeon to the Marine Battalion, as Assessors. Four Students, who had completed the prescribed curriculum, presented themselves for examination, but were not found qualified.

13. In the awarding of Scholarships at the close of last Session it was found that the Fourth Year Students did

Award of Scholarships.

not come up to the standard fixed on for qualification to compete for Scholarships; but this year I am happy to state that the Carnac and Anderson Scholarships, competed for by Students of the Fourth Year, have been awarded to two young men, who have distinguished themselves by their intelligence, their zealous industry, and their possession of the rare quality of careful and patient observation. A Carnac Scholarship, for proficiency in conducting the duties of Clinical Clerk, and in knowledge of Practical Medicine and Pathology, has been awarded to Burjorjee Framjee. An Anderson Scholarship, for proficiency in conducting the duties of Surgical Dresser, and in knowledge of Practical Surgery and Surgical Anatomy, has been awarded to Eduljee Nusserwanjee. Of the three Scholarships offered

3

to Th'rd Year Students, that for the first degree of profi-
ciency in Anatomy and Physiology has been awarded to
J. N. Mendonça; that for the second degree of proficiency
in these subjects, to Surfoodin Sumsoodin; that for Materia
Medica and Practical Pharmacy, to Muncherjee Byramjee.
Of the three Scholarships to Second Year Students, that for
Anatomy, and that for Materia Medica and Practical
Pharmacy, have been awarded to Nusserwanjee. Dhunjeebhoy; but, as he can enjoy the emoluments of only one of
these, the Anatomical Scholarship passes to the Student
who has attained the next degree of proficiency in this subject, Dorabjee Hormusjee; and that for Chemistry, Theoretical and Practical, has been awarded to Furdoonjee Byramjee. Of the First Year Students, Shantaram Wittul
has gained the Scholarship for proficiency in Anatomy;
and Kaikusrao Rustomjee that for proficiency in Chemistry.

14. The Sir Jamsetjee Jejeebhoy Medical Prize of
Sir Jamsetjee Jejeebhoy Prize, and the McLennan Scholarship and Silver Medal, and the Burnes Medal. Rs. 250, and the McLennan
Scholarship and Silver Medal,
open for competition to the
Graduates of the Session, have,
of course, not been awarded; and, owing to the temporary
removal of the Student Apprentices, the Burnes and
McLennan Medals, annually competed for by that Class,
are not awarded.

15. The sum of Rs. 1,800, given by the late Hemabhoy
Hemabhoy Vukhutchund Medal. Vukhutchund of Ahmedabad,
to found a gold Medal bearing
his name, not being sufficient
for the purpose, it is lying at interest in the Government
Treasury.

16. The Prize of Rupees 300 left by the Honorable
The Willoughby Prize. Mr. Willoughby, on his departure for Europe in 1851, never having yet been competed for, that sum has been expended in the purchase of a collection of books of reference for the Students' Reading Room.

17. Donations to the Library have been received from
Donations to the Library and Museum. C. Morehead, Esq., M.D.; T. B. Beatty, Esq. ; Dr. Downes ; M. Thompson, Esq. ; Mr. Burjorjee Dorabjee ; Geographical Society of Bombay ; and Pathological Society of London. And to the Museum, from Dr. Morehead ; Dr. Leith ; Dr. Kearney ; Dr. Ballingall ; Dr. Mead ; Meerza Ali Mahomed, Esq.; Mr. Burjorjee Dorabjee ; and the Curator.

18. At the commencement of the Session a set of first-
Course of Microscopic Demonstrations. rate Microscopes, selected in England by Professor Queckett, arrived ; and a course of Microscopic Demonstrations was delivered by the Professor of Anatomy and Physiology.

19. The Grant College Medical Society has continued
Grant College Medical Society. to hold its regular monthly meetings.

HERBERT GIRAUD, M.D., Edin.,
Acting Principal, Grant Medical College.

APPENDICES .

TO THE

ANNUAL REPORT OF THE GRANT MEDICAL COLLEGE.

TWELFTH YEAR.—SESSION 1857-58.

APPENDIX A.

List of Candidates for Admission as Students into the Grant Medical College, with the Result of the Examinations held on the 21st, 22nd, and 23rd April 1857.

No.	Names.	Caste.	School where Educated.	Qualified or not.	Remarks.
1	Framjee Bomonjee	Parsee	Elphinstone Institution	⎫	
2	Nusserwanjee Jehangeerjee	Ditto	Ditto	⎪	
3	Kaikusrao Rustomjee	Ditto	Ditto	⎪	
4	Burjorjee Byramjee	Ditto	Ditto	⎬ Qualified.	
5	Shantaram Wittul	Shenvi	Ditto	⎪	
6	A. de Souza	Portuguese	Ditto	⎪	
7	J. A. Hannah	East Indian	Ditto	⎭	
8	Dinsha Herjibhai	Parsee	Ditto	⎫	
9	Hormusjee Dadabhoy	Ditto	Ditto	⎬	
10	Mahadew Moreshwur	Brahmin	Kolapore English School	⎭	
11	Wittul Narrayen	Ditto	Ditto		
12	Gunnesh Govind	Ditto	Poona College	⎫	
13	Vajinath Anant	Purbhoo	Elphinstone Institution	⎪	
14	Crustnath Balcrustna	Ditto	Ditto	⎬ Not Qualified.	
15	Jahangeer Hormusjee	Parsee	Ditto	⎪	
16	Shamrao Juggonnath	Purbhoo	Purbhoo Seminary	⎪	
17	Gunput Kessow	Brahmin	Free General Assembly Inst.	⎭	

HERBERT GIRAUD,
Acting Principal, Grant Medical College.

APPENDIX B.

List of Students in Attendance in the Grant Medical College, during the Session 1857-58.

No.	Names.	Caste.	Age on Admission.	Native Town.	In what, School Educated.	Date of Admission.	Remarks.
	Free.						
1	Jejeebhoy Bazonjee	Parsee	18	Bombay	Elphinstone Institution	15th June 1854	
2	J. N. Mendouca	Portuguese	17	Ditto	American Mission Inst.	15th June 1855	
3	Cowasjee Hormusjee	Parsee	17	Ditto	Elphinstone Institution	Ditto.	
4	Ruslonjee Hormusjee	Ditto	18	Ditto	Ditto	Ditto.	
5	Cowasjee Mendozjue	Ditto	17	Ditto	Ditto	Ditto.	
6	Dadabhoy Jamasjee	Ditto	18	Ditto	Parsee B. Institution	Ditto.	
7	Nanabhoy Eduljee	Ditto	19	Ditto	Elphinstone Institution	16th June 1850	
8	Abdool Kurrim Lukmonjee	Borah	17	Ditto	Ditto	Ditto.	
9	Ambaram Kuvalram	Bania	19	Surat	Ditto	Ditto.	
10	Hormusjee Pestonjee	Parsee	19	Bombay	Ditto	Ditto.	Withdrawn.
11	Soonderrow Bha-kerjee	Purbhoo	17	Ditto	Ditto	Ditto.	Ditto.
12	Hurreechund Gopal	Casar	16	Ditto	General Assembly Inst.	Ditto.	Ditto.
13	Pestonjee Nowrojee	Parsee	19	Ditto	Elphinstone Institution	Ditto.	
14	Kaikusrao Rustonjee	Ditto	18	Ditto	Ditto	15th June 1867	
15	Shantaram Wittul	Shenvi	19	Ditto	Ditto	Ditto.	
	Stipendiary.						
16	Jumnadas Hurgovindas	Bania	18	Surat	Elphinstone Institution	15th June 1853	Withdrawn.
17	Bhikajee Amroot	Brahmin	18	Aukloas	Poona College	Ditto.	

No.	Names.	Caste.	Age on Admission.	Native Town.	In what School Educated.	Date of Admission.	Remarks.
	Stipendiary—(cont.)						
18	Wamon Wassoodave	Brahmin	18	Poona	Poona College	15th June 1853	
19	Rustomjee Cowasjee	Parsee	21	Surat	Educated by Mr. Green	Ditto.	
20	A. P. de Andrade	Portuguese	20	Goa	Free Church Institution	Ditto.	
21	Ramchundra Narayen	Sonar	17	Bombay	Free Genl. Assembly Inst.	15th June 1855	
22	Eduljee Nusserwanjee	Parsee	17	Ditto	Elphinstone Institution	Ditto.	
23	Huree Vishnoo	Brahmin	17	Rutnacherry	Ditto	Ditto.	
24	Burjorjee Franjee	Parsee	17	Bombay	Ditto	Ditto.	
25	Pestonjee Muncherjee	Ditto	18	Ditto	Parsee Benevolent Inst.	Ditto.	
26	Pestonjee Bomanjee	Ditto	19	Surat	Ditto	Ditto.	
27	Manockjee Aderjee	Ditto	18	Bombay	Elphinstone Institution	Ditto.	
28	Dossabhoy Pestonjee	Ditto	17	Broach	Broach Govt. Eng. School	Ditto.	
29	Heerajee Eduljee	Ditto	18	Bombay	Elphinstone Institution	Ditto.	
30	Muncherjee Byramjee	Ditto	19	Ditto	Ditto	Ditto.	
31	Jamsetjee Byramjee	Ditto	18	Ditto	Ditto	Ditto.	
32	Byramjee Naorosjee	Ditto	18	Ditto	Ditto	Ditto.	
33	Surfoodin Nunsoodin	Borah	17	Ditto	Ditto	Ditto.	
34	Nusserwanjee Dhunjeebhoy	Parsee	19	Surat	Ditto	16th June 1856	
35	Dorabjee Hormusjee	Ditto	19	Ditto	Ditto	Ditto.	
36	Franjee Shapoorjee	Ditto	19	Bombay	Ditto	Ditto.	
37	Furdoonjee Byramjee	Ditto	19	Ditto	Ditto	Ditto.	
38	P. A. de Nazareth	Portuguese	19	Goa	Poona Free Church Inst.	Ditto.	
39	Franjee Bomonjee	Parsee	17	Bombay	Elphinstone Institution	15th June 1857	
40	Nusserwanjee Jehangerjee	Ditto	18	Ditto	Ditto	Ditto.	
41	Burjorjee Byramjee	Ditto	17	Ditto	Ditto	Ditto.	

HERBERT GIRAUD,
Acting Principal, Grant Medical College.

APPENDIX C.

GRANT MEDICAL COLLEGE.

SESSION 1857-58.

SUMMER TERM.

From 15th June to 1st November.

LECTURES.

On Monday the 15th June, the Introductory Lecture will be delivered by Dr. Ballingall, at 11 o'clock.

ANATOMY. *Dr. T. M. Lownds*	{ Monday.... Wednesday. Saturday .. }	at 1 P. M.
CHEMISTRY. *Dr. H. Giraud*	{ Tuesday .. Thursday.. }	at 12 o'clock.
PHYSIOLOGY. *Dr. T. M. Lownds*...........	Tuesday ..	at 2 P. M.
MATERIA MEDICA. *Mr. G. Seaward*	{ Monday.... Wednesday }	at 11 A. M.
BOTANY. *Dr. H. Giraud*	{ Monday.... Wednesday. }	at 12 o'clock.
PRINCIPLES AND PRACTICE OF MEDICINE. *Dr. C. Morehead*	{ Monday.... Wednesday. Friday .... }	at 2 P. M.
SURGERY. *Dr. G. Ballingall*	{ Tuesday.... Thursday .. Friday .... }	at 1 P. M.
OPHTHALMIC SURGERY. *Mr. H. J. Carter*............	Friday	at 11 A. M.

4

MIDWIFERY. Mr. C. Mead...............	{ Monday.... Wednesday. } at 3 P. M.
MEDICAL JURISPRUDENCE. Dr. W. Campbell	{ Tuesday .. Thursday .. } at 3 P. M.
CLINICAL SURGERY. Dr. G. Ballingall	Thursday ....at 11 A. M.
CLINICAL MEDICINE. Dr. C. Morehead	Tuesday ....at 11 A. M.
PRACTICAL CHEMISTRY. Dr. H. Giraud	Friday.. from 11 to 1 o'clock.
OPERATIVE SURGERY. Dr. G. Ballingall	{ Tuesday .... Friday...... } at 12 o'clock.

HOSPITAL ATTENDANCE.

Clinical Medical Ward	Daily, at 7 A. M.
Clinical Surgical Ward	Do. at 8 A. M.
Clinical Midwifery Ward	Do. at 4 P. M.
Dispensary Practice................	Do. at 8 A. M.

The 1st and 2nd Year Students will attend the Hospital daily at 7 A. M. in rotation, for periods of two months, and will be engaged in compounding and dispensing Medicine.

EXAMINATIONS.

ANATOMY...............	Friday, at 3 P. M.
CHEMISTRY..............	Saturday, at 11 A. M.
MATERIA MEDICA	Saturday, at 3 P. M.
BOTANY	Saturday, at 12 o'clock.
PHYSIOLOGY	Thursday, at 2 P. M.
SURGERY...............	Wednesday, at 12 o'clock.
OPHTHALMIC SURGERY....	Saturday, at 11 A. M.
MEDICINE	Saturday, at 2 P. M.
MEDICAL JURISPRUDENCE .	Saturday, at 3 P. M.
MIDWIFERY	Friday, at 3 P. M.

During the hours when not engaged in the Lecture-room, the Students will be occupied in reading and note-taking in the Reading-room.

WINTER TERM.

From 1st November to 15th March.

The Lectures and Examinations will be on the same days and at the same hours as during the *Summer Term*, with the exception that there will not be any Lectures upon Ophthalmic Surgery and Botany, those subjects being finished in the *Summer Term*. Practical Toxicology will be taught in the Laboratory every Monday, from 11 to 1 o'clock.

PRACTICAL ANATOMY.

The Dissecting Season will be from the 1st November to the 15th March.

1. Each *Junior* Student will be expected to study, practically, during this period, under the superintendence of the Professor of Anatomy and his Assistant, the Anatomy of the Ligaments, Muscles, and the principal Blood-vessels and Nerves.

2. Each *Senior* Student who has not passed the First Certificate Examination will, in like manner, be expected to examine *fully* and *carefully*, the Anatomy of the Arteries, Nerves, Viscera, and the more important Surgical regions.

3. 4th, 5th, and 6th Year Students will be expected to study, under the superintendence of the Professor of Surgery, the various Surgical regions, and to connect with such examination the performance of Surgical operations.

4. To ensure a compliance with these Regulations, a Register will be regularly kept by the Professors of Anatomy and Surgery, according to a prescribed form. These Registers will be laid before the Examiners at the First Certificate and Final Examinations.

5. A Roll will be called in the Dissecting-room at 11, 2, and 4 o'clock.

6. During the Winter Season, the 2nd and 3rd Year Students will only attend those Examinations in Anatomy and Physiology which are held on Thursday and Friday.

ROLL-CALLS.

The College hours are from 10 A. M. to 4 P. M. A Roll-call will take place before the commencement of each Lecture and Examination, as well as in the Clinical Wards.

From the 15th March to the 15th April the Examination will be held for Diplomas, Honours, and the classification of the Students.

Order of the Lectures and Examinations during the Day.

	11 to 12 A. M.	12 to 1 P. M.	1 to 2 P. M.	2 to 3 P. M.	3 to 4 P. M.
MONDAY.	Materia Medica.	Botany.	Anatomy.	Medicine.	Midwifery.
TUESDAY.	Clinical Medicine. *Examination Materia Medica.*	Operative Surgery. Chemistry.	Surgery.	Physiology.	Medical Jurisprudence.
WEDNESDAY	Materia Medica.	Botany. Examination Surgery.	Anatomy.	Medicine.	Midwifery.
THURSDAY.	Clinical Surgery. *Examination Materia Medica.*	Chemistry.	Surgery.	Examination Physiology.	Medical Jurisprudence.
FRIDAY.	Practical Chemistry. Ophthalmic Surgery.	Operative Surgery. Practical Chemistry.	Surgery.	Medicine.	Examination Anatomy. Examination Midwifery.
SATURDAY.	Examination Chemistry. Examination Ophthalmic Surgery.	Examination Botany.	Anatomy.	Examination Medicine.	Examination Medical Jurisprudence. Examination Materia Medica.

C. MOREHEAD, M.D.,
Principal.

APPENDIX D.

Abstract of Roll-calls of Students, for the Session 1857-58.

Names.	Absent.	Leave.	Sick.	Total.	No. of Roll-calls.
Bhicajee Amroot	..	4	46	50	
Wamon Wassoodave	5	6	81	92	
A. P. de Andrade	..	..	..	..	1524
Rustomjee Cowasjee	1	6	11	18	
Eduljee Nasserwanjee	..	6	48	54	
Burjorjee Framjee	..	12	33	45	
Pestonjee Bomonjee	12	8	56	76	
Ramchundra Narrayen	145	5	149	299	1426
Manockjee Aderjee	1	12	37	50	
Hurry Vishnoo	..	4	338	342	
Pestonjee Muncherjee	..	20	38	58	
Jejeebhoy Bazunjee	..	8	51	59	
Muncherjee Byramjee	..	6	9	15	
J. N. Mendonça	3	..	190	193	
Byramjee Nowrojee	..	9	35	44	
Surfoodeen Sumsoodin	2	8	60	70	
Dossabhoy Pestonjee	1	10	47	58	
Rustomjee Hormusjee	1	..	26	27	1892
Heerajee Eduljee	1	11	57	69	
Dadabhoy Jamasjee	1	8	117	126	
Jamsetjee Byramjee	22	11	69	102	
Cowasjee Hormusjee	1	..	..	1	
Cowasjee Mendozjee	..	8	129	137	
Furdoonjee Byramjee	..	13	29	42	
Ambaram Kavalram	8	16	17	41	
Nusserwanjee Dhunjeebhoy	..	8	3	11	

Names.	Absent.	Leave.	Sick.	Total.	No. of Roll-calls.
Dorabjee Hormusjee	..	1	..	1	
Framjee Shapoorjee	1	..	..	1	
P. A. de Nazareth	9	·17	256	282	
Abdool Kurrim Luckmonjee	2	11	15	28	1211
Hureechund Gopall	..	17	127	144	
Nanabhoy Eduljee	1	20	11	32	
Soonderrow Bhaskerjee	..	3	49	52	
Pestonjee Nowrojee............	..	5	..	5	
Hormusjee Pestonjee	..	5	131	136	
Framjee Bomonjee	5	5	7	17	
Nusserwanjee Jehangeerjee......	..	10	34	44	
Kaikusrao Rustomjee..........	..	9	..	9	838
Burjorjee Byramjee............	..	..	73	73	
Shautaram Wittul	14	16	31	61	

HERBERT GIRAUD,
Acting Principal, Grant Medical College.

APPENDIX E.

Return of Student Apprentices who have attended the College during the Session 1857-58.

No.	Names.	Age at Admission.	Date of joining the College.	Remarks.
1	Charles Chreswick............	17	15th June 1855.	
2	Minguel St. Francis	19	,, ,,	
3	Adam A. Byrne..............	18	,, ,,	
4	Ahmed Khan................	21	,, ,,	
5	John L. Tiernan.............	18	16th June 1856.	
6	Andrew de Rozario	19	,, ,,	
7	Rama Succaram.............	20	,, ,,	
8	John Wynne................	18	,, ,,	
9	Roque de Silva	19	,, ,,	

No.	Names.	Age at Admission.	Date of joining the College.	Remarks.
10	Augustus de Souza	18	15th June 1856.	
11	George Strip	21	„ „	
12	George Williams	18	„ „	
13	M. P. O'Shaughnessy	19	„ „	Resigned.
14	Patrick Clancy	19	„ „	
15	G. Telly	18	15th June 1857.	
16	A. de Silva	18	„ „	
17	John Law	17	„ „	
18	S. Gillon	18	„ „	
19	J. A. Kyte	17	„ „	
20	David Cooper	22	„ „	
21	James Gurnett	18	„ „	

HERBERT GIRAUD,
Acting Principal, Grant Medical College.

APPENDIX F.

Return of Hospital Assistants, who have attended the College during the Session 1857-58.

No.	Names.	Rank.	Date of joining the College.
1	P. A. de Crostos..	2nd Hospital Assist.	15th June 1857.
2	Ramchunder Go-vind.	1st ditto........	— November 1856.
3	Manajee Sonowla..	1st ditto........	15th October 1855.
4	Ramchunder Shree-dhur.	2nd ditto........	15th June 1855.
5	Gungajee Nursoo..	2nd ditto........	29th July 1854.

HERBERT GIRAUD,
Acting Principal, Grant Medical College.

APPENDIX G.

NUMBERS IN ATTENDANCE IN THE COLLEGE.

STUDENTS.

Remained at the close of last Session. 36
Admitted at commencement of this Session. 5
                                                    ——41

STUDENT APPRENTICES.

Remained at the close of last Session. . . . . ' 14
Admitted at commencement of this Session. . . . . ' 7
                                                    ——21

HOSPITAL ASSISTANTS.

Number attending during the Session 5

                            Total. 67

HERBERT GIRAUD,
Acting Principal, Grant Medical College.

APPENDIX H.

STATEMENT OF THE NUMBERS ATTENDING THE SEVERAL COURSES OF LECTURES.

ANATOMY.

Students.. 28
Hospital Assistants 2
Student Apprentices.............................. 17

Total.... 47

CHEMISTRY.

Students.. 28
Hospital Assistants 2
Student Apprentices.............................. 7

Total.... 37

MATERIA MEDICA.

Students.. 23
Hospital Assistants 2
Student Apprentices.............................. 7

Total.... 32

PHYSIOLOGY.

Students.. 23
Hospital Assistants 2
Student Apprentices.............................. 10

Total.... 35

Principles and Practice of Medicine.

Students	24
Hospital Assistants	3
Student Apprentices	14
Total....	41

Surgery.

Students	24
Hospital Assistants	3
Student Apprentices	14
Total....	41

Midwifery.

Students	13
Hospital Assistants	3
Student Apprentices	4
Total....	20

Medical Jurisprudence.

Students	13
Hospital Assistants	3
Student Apprentices	4
Total....	20

Ophthalmic Surgery.

Students	13
Student Apprentices	4
Total....	17

HERBERT GIRAUD,
Acting Principal, Grant Medical College.

APPENDIX I.

Return of the Sick treated in the Clinical Medical Ward of the Jamsetjee Jejeebhoy Hospital in the Session 1857-58, from 15th June 1857 to 15th March 1858.

Names of Diseases.	Number Admitted.	Number Discharged.	Died.	Total.	Remarks.
Febricula	1	1	..	1	
FEVERS. Intermittent — Quotidian, Simple	24	2	..		
,, c. Pneumonia	2	2	..		
,, Bronchitis	1	1	..		
,, Enlarged Spleen	4	4	..		
,, Dysentery	1	1	..		
,, Jaundice	1	..	1		
Tertian, Simple	2	2	..		
Quartan, ,,	1	1	..		
Remittent — Simple	6	6	..		
Complicated c. Pneumonia	12	9	3	36	

Names of Diseases.		Number Admitted.	Number Discharged.	Died.	Total.	Remarks.
FEVERS. Remittent	Complicated c. Bronchitis	3	3	:	26	
	„ Hepatitis	2	1	1		
	„ Jaundice	2	2	:		
	„ Enlarged Spleen	1	1	:		
DISEASES OF THE NERVOUS SYSTEM	Hemiplegia	5	5	:	13	
	Paraplegia	3	2	1		
	Paralysis	1	1	:		
	Delirium Tremens	1	1	:		
	Tetanus	2	2	:		
	Chorea	1	1	:		
DISEASES OF AIR-PASSAGES AND LUNGS	Pneumonia	11	8	3	28	
	Bronchitis	1	1	:		
	Phthisis Pulmonalis	15	10	5		
	Asthma	1	1	:		
DISEASES OF HEART AND VASCULAR SYSTEM	Disease of Mitral Valve	2	2	:	3	
	„ Aortic Valve	1	:	1		
DISEASES OF LIVER AND VISCERA	Hepatitis, Acute	6	4	2	11	
	„ Chronic	3	3	:		
	Jaundice	1	1	:		
	Enlargement of Spleen	1	1	:		

DISEASES OF STOMACH AND BOWELS	Dysentery, Acute	11	9	2
	" Chronic	13	10	3
	Gastritis	1	1	..
	Diarrhœa	3	3	..
	Dyspepsia	1	1	.. 29
DISEASES OF URINARY ORGANS	Bright's Disease	3	2	1 3
DISEASES OF GENERAL SYSTEM	Rheumatism	7	6	1
	Syphilis	2	2	..
	Scurvy	2	2	..
	Cachexia	3	3	.. 14
DROPSIES	General Dropsy	2	1	1
	Ascites	1	1	.. 3
		2	2	.. 2
Tænia		..	..	..
Total,				169

T. M. LOWNDS, M.D.,

Acting Professor of Medicine, Grant Medical College.

Statement, showing the Classes of Disease treated in the Jamsetjee Jejeebhoy Hospital, from 1st January to 31st December 1857.

	MALES							FEMALES							TOTAL						
	Remained	Admitted	Total	Discharged	Died	Remaining	Total	Remained	Admitted	Total	Discharged	Died	Remaining	Total	Remained	Admitted	Total	Discharged	Died	Remaining	Total
I. Fevers	35	584	619	515	68	36	610	5	105	110	69	14	7	110	40	689	729	604	89	43	729
II. Eruptive Fevers	..	19	19	12	0	1	19	..	9	9	6	3	..	9	..	28	28	18	0	1	28
III. Epidemic Diseases	2	164	106	54	112	..	166	..	28	28	11	17	..	28	2	192	194	65	129	..	194
IV. Diseases of the Nervous System	2	277	279	211	50	8	270	..	53	53	43	7	3	53	2	330	332	254	66	12	332
V. Diseases of the Air-Passages and Lungs	14	239	253	130	93	8	253	6	61	67	41	22	4	67	20	300	320	191	117	12	320
VI. Diseases of the Heart and Vascular System	..	18	18	0	6	3	18	1	11	12	5	6	1	12	..	18	18	9	8	1	18
VII. Diseases of the Liver and Spleen	5	90	95	53	37	3	95	1	11	12	6	5	1	12	6	101	107	60	43	4	107
VIII. Diseases of the Stomach and Bowels	45	584	629	354	242	1	629	4	189	193	94	88	11	193	48	773	821	448	330	43	821
IX. Diseases of the Nose, Ear, Mouth, and Fauces	1	9	10	9	..	1	10	1	4	5	3	2	..	5	2	13	15	12	2	1	15
X. Diseases of the Eye	3	55	58	57	..	1	58	..	22	64	22	..	2	64	3	77	80	79	..	1	80
XI. Diseases of the Integumentary Tissues	30	481	511	431	32	48	511	3	61	64	60	2	2	64	33	542	575	491	34	50	575
XII. Diseases of the Bones and Joints	2	26	28	24	4	..	28	..	6	6	6	..	..	6	2	32	34	30	3	1	34
XIII. Diseases of the Urinary & Reproductive Organs	23	334	357	335	..	18	357	1	81	82	75	..	5	82	24	415	439	410	6	23	439
XIV. Diseases of the Rectum and Anus	1	17	18	18	..	..	18	1	3	3	3	..	..	3	..	20	20	20	..	..	21
XV. Diseases of the General System	38	614	614	563	43	38	614	2	132	131	104	20	10	131	40	738	778	697	63	48	778
XVI. Dropsies	..	23	25	14	5	3	25	2	13	11	7	5	2	14	3	86	89	81	13	5	89
XVII. Entozoa	4	68	68	61	..	3	64	..	1	1	1	..	..	1	4	65	60	60	..	2	60
XVIII. Tumours	..	9	9	5	..	..	9	..	3	3	3	..	..	3	..	9	9	8	..	..	9
XIX. Fractures, Dislocations, Wounds, and Injuries	22	340	362	318	20	24	362	3	92	95	90	1	4	95	25	432	457	408	21	28	457
XX. Congenital Malformations	2	..	2	2	..	..	2	3	1	1	..	..	..	1	3	3	3	3	..	..	3
Total....	226	3940	4106	3202	735	229	4166	29	873	902	664	189	40	902	255	4815	5008	3966	924	278	5008

HERBERT GIRAUD,

Acting Surgeon, J. J. Hospital.

Note of the Principal Classes of Disease treated at the Jamsetjee Jejeebhoy Hospital Dispensary, from 1st January to 31st December 1857, arranged according to Sex.

Diseases.	Males.	Females.	Children.	Total.
Fevers	1,271	434	526	2,231
Affections of the Stomach and Bowels	1,175	485	822	2,482
Affections of the Air-Passages...	546	310	584	1,440
Rheumatic Affections	632	277	5	914
Venereal Affections	1,409	137	1	1,547
Skin Diseases	1,653	299	575	2,527
Uterine Diseases	..	110	..	110

Total Number treated at the Dispensary, arranged according to Caste and Sex.

Caste.	Males.	Females and Children
Christians	719	652
Mussulmans	3,620	1,868
Hindoos ....:	3,678	1,580
Parsees	1,059	1,539
Total....	9,076	5,639
Grand Total....	14,715	

HERBERT GIRAUD,
Acting Surgeon, Jamsetjee Jejeebhoy Hospital.

6

APPENDIX J.

Register of Cases treated in the Clinical Surgical Ward, during the Session 1857-58.

Diseases.	Admitted.	Discharged.	Died.	Remarks.
Abscess	4	4	...	
Burn	1	1	...	
Cicatrix of Burn	1	1	...	Divided, with improvement.
Concussion of Brain	5	5	...	
Diseases of Bones { Caries	3	3	...	
Necrosis	1	1	...	Suspected fracture of base in one.
Osteitis	3	3	...	Amputation of leg in one, of foot in another.
Diseases of Rectum and Anus { Fistula in Ano	2	2	...	
Haemorrhoids, Internal	1	1	...	
Calculus, Urethral	1	1	...	
" Vesical	6	5	1	Lithotomy in all.
Fungus Testis	1	1	...	
Diseases of Urinary and Genital Organs { Gonorrhoea	1	1	...	
Haematocele	3	3	...	
Hydrocele	2	2	...	

				Remarks
Hypertrophy of Scrotum	2	2	:	Removal in both.
Phymosis	1	1	:	
Stricture of Urethra	4	4	1	Laceration and compression of brain.
Fractures — Simple — Skull	1	1	1	
Bones of Face	2	2	:	
Clavicle	2	3	:	
Humerus	4	4	:	
Fore-arm	2	2	:	
Cervix Femoris	4	4	:	
Femur	1	1	:	
Patella	2	2	:	
Leg	1	2	1	Died of Phthisis.
Compound & Compound Comminuted — Lower Jaw	2	1	2	Both died of Tetanus.
Humerus	5	5	1	Death from Gangrene, another removed dying.
Fore-arm	3	3	:	
Hand	8	8	:	
Femur	3	3	2	Secondary amputation in one.
Leg	8	3	5	Primary amputation in two, secondary in one.
Scapula and Ribs	1	1	:	
Fistula in Perineo	1	1	1	Successful operation in both.
Gangrene of Foot (dry)	2	2	:	
Harelip	2	2	2	Amputation.
Supernumerary Finger and Toes	1	1	:	
Syphilis, Primary	2	2	:	
,, Secondary	5	4	1	Death from abscess of brain.
Tumours, Malignant	4	4	:	
,, Non-malignant	3	3	:	
Ulcers	3	3	:	Foot amputated in one.
Strangulated Inguinal Hernia	1	1	:	
Tetanus, Idiopathic	1	1	1	Operation, removed dying.
Wounds — Incised of throat	1	1	:	
,,	1	1	:	

Diseases.	Admitted.	Dis-charged.	Died.	Remarks.
Wounds { Contused and lacerated	11	9	2	
Punctured	1	1	..	
Penetrating of Abdomen with protrusion	1	..	1	Died of Gangrene.
Contu..on	2	2	..	
Total........	128	107	21	

(Signed) G. R. BALLINGALL,
Professor of Surgery.

*Table of Capital and Minor Operations, performed in pre-
sence of or by the Students, during the Session* 1857-58.

Amputation of Thigh 2
Ditto of Leg. 3
Ditto of Foot at ankle. 1
Ditto of Fore-arm 2
Ditto of Fingers and Toes 5
Lithotomy 6
Excision of Scrotum 2
Hare-lip operation 2
Passing Catheters and Sounds 55
Opening Abscesses, &c........................... 231
Tapping Hydrocele 59
Extracting Teeth 152
Circumcision 8
Removal of Sequestra........................... 2
Ditto of Polypi 4
Ditto of Calculus from Urethra 2
Ditto of Hæmorrhoids 2
Ditto of Tumours 5
Operation for Strangulated Hernia 1
Reducing dislocated Jaw 2

Total.. 546

(Signed) G. R. BALLINGALL,
Professor of Surgery.

APPENDIX K.

Cases treated in the Obstetric Institution, from 1st January to 31st December 1857.

Parturition, &c.	Caste.	Result to Mothers.	Result to Children.	Sex of Children.
Natural........ 34	Christians .. 28	Died........ 2	Born alive.... 27	Male........... 29
Difficult........ 3	Mussulmans. 5	Discharged .. 44	Born dead. .. 11	Female........... 9
Preternatural .. 1	Hindoos 3			
Abortions 4	Parsees...... 10			
Uterine Diseases. 6				
Total.. 48	Total .. 46	Total.. 46	Total.. 38	Total.. 38

(Signed)   C. C. MEAD,
Professor of Midwifery.

APPENDIX L.

GRANT MEDICAL COLLEGE.

THE ANNUAL EXAMINATIONS at the Grant Medical College will commence on Tuesday, the 9th March, and be conducted in the following manner : —

I.—EXAMINATION OF CANDIDATES FOR " FIRST EXAMINATION" CERTIFICATES.

Tuesday, 9th March.—Practical Anatomy.

Wednesday, 10th.—Written examination in Anatomy and in Physiology.

Thursday, 11th.—Written examination in Chemistry.

Friday, 12th.—Oral examination in Anatomy.

Saturday, 13th.—Written examination in Materia Medica.

Monday, 15th.—Oral examination in Chemistry.

Tuesday, 16th.—Oral examination in Materia Medica, and in Botany.

Wednesday 17th.—Oral examination in Physiology.

Thursday, 18th.—Practical Chemistry and Pharmacy.

II.—EXAMINATION OF CANDIDATES FOR THE DIPLOMA OF GRADUATE, CONDUCTED BY THE GOVERNMENT EXAMINER AND ASSESSORS.

Friday, 19th March.—Written examination in Medicine.

Saturday, 20th.—Written examination in Surgery.

Wednesday, 24th.—Oral examination in Medicine.

Friday, 26th.—Oral and practical examination in Surgery.

Saturday, 27th.—Written examination in Midwifery.

Monday, 29th.—Written examination in Medical Jurisprudence.

Wednesday, 31st.—Oral examination in Midwifery.

Saturday, 3rd April.—Oral and practical examination in Medical Jurisprudence.

[Examinations in the J. J. Hospital in Clinical Medicine and in Clinical Surgery were commenced in February.]

III.—EXAMINATION OF COLLEGE STUDENTS.

1st and 2nd Year Students.

Tuesday, 9th March.—Practical Anatomy.

Wednesday, 10th.—Written examination in Anatomy and in Physiology.

Thursday, 11th.—Written examination in Chemistry.

Saturday, 13th.—Oral examination in Anatomy and Physiology.

Tuesday, 16th.—Oral examination in Materia Medica and in Botany.

Wednesday, 17th.—Oral examination in Chemistry.

Thursday, 18th.—Practical Chemistry and Pharmacy.

3rd and 4th Year Students.

Friday, 19th March.—Written examination in Medicine and Surgery.

Saturday, 20th.—Oral examination. in Medicine, Surgery, and Ophthalmic Surgery.

Saturday, 27th.—Oral examination in Midwifery and Medical Jurisprudence.

The 3rd Year Students who do not present themselves for examination for "First Examination" Certificates will be examined in Anatomy, Physiology, and Materia Medica, with the 2nd Year Students.

IV.—EXAMINATION FOR SCHOLARSHIPS AND PRIZES NOTIFIED ON 10TH NOVEMBER 1857.

4th Year Students who have qualified for "First Examination" Certificates.—Carnac and Anderson Scholarships, on 19th March, in the Dissecting Room ; 22nd, 24th, 25th, and 26th March in the Clinical Wards.

Graduates.—Sir Jamsetjee Jejeebhoy Prize and McLennan Scholarship, on 6th, 7th, and 8th April.

The Examination on each day will commence at 11 o'clock A. M., and the attendance of Medical Gentlemen, and others interested in Medical Education, will be very acceptable.

HERBERT GIRAUD, M.D.,   W. ARBUCKLE, M.D.,
    Acting Principal.   Government Examiner.

Bombay, 1st March 1858.

SCHEME OF EXAMINATIONS,

Session 1857-58.

42

Scheme of Grant College

Dates.	" First Certificato" Examination.	Diplomn Examination.	
Mar.			
Tuesday 9	Practical Anatomy........	....	
Wednesday 10	Anatomy and Physiology,W.	....	{
Thursday 11	Chemistry, W.	....	
Friday.......... 12	Anatomy, O.	....	
Saturday 13	Materia Medica, W.	....	{
Monday 15	Chemistry, O...........	....	
Tuesday 16	Materia Medica & Botany,O.	....	{
Wednesday 17	Physiology, O...........	....	
Thursday........ 18	{ Practical Chemistry and (Pharmacy	....	{
Friday 19	....	Medicine, W.	
Saturday 20	....	Surgery, W...........	
Monday 22	....	....	
Wednesday 24	....	Medicine, O...........	
Thursday 25	....	....	
Friday 26	....	{ Surgery, Oral and (Practical	
Saturday 27	....	Midwifery, W........	
Monday 29	....	Medical Jurisprud., W.	
Tuesday 30	....	....	
Wednesday 31	....	Midwifery, O.	
Apr.			
Saturday 3	....	{ Medical Jurisprudence, (Oral and Practical.	
Monday 5	....	....	
Tuesday 6	....	....	
Wednesday 7	....	....	
Thursday 8	....	....	

W. Written examination.

Examinations.—Session 1857-58.

COLLEGE STUDENTS.		SCHOLARSHIPS AND PRIZES.	
1st and 2nd Year.	3rd and 4th Year.	Graduates.	4th Year Students.
Practical Anatomy. Anatomy and Physiology, W. Chemistry, W. .... Anatomy and Physiology, O. .... Materia Medica and Botany, O. Chemistry, O. Practical Chemistry and Pharmacy.	-		
....	{ Medicine and Surgery, W ..	{	{ Carnac & Anderson, Dissecting Room.
....	{ Medicine, Surg., and Ophthal. Surgery, O.		
....	....	....	{ Carnac & Anderson, Clinical Wards.
....	....	....	Do. do.
....	....	....	Do. 'do.
....	....	....	Do. do.
....	{ Midwifery, and Medical Jurisprudence, O.		
....	....	{ Sir J. J. Prize and McLennan Scholarship.	
....	....	Do. do.	
....	....	Do. do.	

O. Oral or *vivâ voce* examination.

APPENDIX M.

Result of First Certificate Examination.—Session 1857-58.

No. of Years' Study	Names	Anatomy	Physiology	Materia Medica	Botany	Chemistry	Practical Chemistry	Practical Anatomy	Practical Pharmacy	Remarks
6	Rustomjee Cowasjee	Qualified.	Qualified.	Qualified.	Qualified.	Qualified.	Qualified.	Qualified.	Qualified.	Qualified.
4	Jejeebhoy Bazonjee	Qualified.	Qualified.	Qualified.	Qualified.	Qualified.	Qualified.	Qualified.	Qualified.	Qualified.
4	Manockjee Aderjee	Qualified.	Qualified.	Qualified.	Qualified.	Qualified.	Qualified.	Qualified.	Qualified.	Qualified.
4	Pestonjee Bomanjee	Qualified.	Qualified.	Qualified.	Qualified.	Qualified.	Qualified.	Qualified.	Qualified.	Qualified.
4	Huree Vishno	Qualified.	Qualified.	Qualified.	Qualified.	Qualified.	Qualified.	Qualified.	Qualified.	Qualified.
4	Pestonjee Muncherjee	Qualified.	Qualified.	Qualified.	Qualified.	Qualified.	Qualified.	Not qual.	Not qual.	Qualified.
4	Ramchundra Narrayen	Not qualified.	Not qualified.	Not qualified.	Not qualified.	Not qualified.	Not qual.	Not qual.	Not qual.	Not qualified.
3	Muncherjee Byramjee	Qualified.	Qualified.	Qualified.	Qualified.	Qualified.	Qualified.	Qualified.	Qualified.	Qualified.
3	J. N. Mendonça	Qualified.	Qualified.	Qualified.	Qualified.	Qualified.	Qualified.	Qualified.	Qualified.	Qualified.
3	Byramjee Naorosjee	Qualified.	Qualified.	Qualified.	Qualified.	Qualified.	Qualified.	Qualified.	Qualified.	Qualified.
3	Surfoodin Sumsoodin	Qualified.	Qualified.	Qualified.	Qualified.	Qualified.	Qualified.	Qualified.	Qualified.	Qualified.
3	Dossabhoy Pestonjee	Qualified.	Qualified.	Qualified.	Qualified.	Qualified.	Qualified.	Qualified.	Qualified.	Qualified.
3	Rustomjee Hormusjee	Qualified.	Not qualified.	Qualified.	Qualified.	Qualified.	Not qual.	Qualified.*	Qualified.	Not qualified.
3	Heerjee Eduljee	Qualified.	Qualified.	Qualified.	Qualified.	Qualified.	Qualified.	Qualified.*	Qualified.	Qualified.
3	Dadabhoy Jamasjee	Not qualified.	Not qualified.	Not qualified.	Not qualified.	Not qualified.	Not qual.	Not qual.	Qualified.	Not qualified.
3	Jamasjee Byramjee	Qualified.	Qualified.	Qualified.	Qualified.	Qualified.	Qualified.	Qualified.	Qualified.	Qualified.
3	Cowasjee Hormusjee	Qualified.	Not qualified.	Qualified.	Qualified.	Qualified.	Not qual.	Not qual.	Qualified.	Not qualified.
3	Cowasjee Mendosjee	Not qualified.	Not qualified.	Not qualified.	Not qualified.	Not qualified.	Qualified.	Qualified.	Qualified.	Not qualified.

HERBERT GIRAUD,

Acting Principal.

APPENDIX N.

FIRST CERTIFICATE EXAMINATION.

ANATOMY.

1. Describe the origin, course, and distribution of the external carotid artery.

2. Describe the articulation between the astragalus, and the os calcis: describing particularly each articulating surface, ligament, and synovial membrane.

3. Describe in detail the distribution of the 8th pair of cranial nerves.

PHYSIOLOGY.

1. Describe the arrangement of Glisson's capsule, and the secreting structure of the liver.

2. State what is known respecting the composition and uses of the bile.

3. Describe the function or functions of the 8th pair of cranial nerves.

T. M. LOWNDS, M.D.,
Professor of Anatomy and Physiology.

March 10th, 1858.

CHEMISTRY.

1. State the law of equivalent composition by weight and volume. Illustrate it by examples ; and explain it on the atomic hypothesis.

2. Explain the phenomena of the generating and of the decomposing cell of a voltaic battery.

3. What is the composition of ferro-cyanide of potassium? and what its action on metallic salts generally, and particularly on those of iron?

4. The preparation, composition, and chemical relations of oxalic acid.

HERBERT GIRAUD, M.D.,
Professor of Chemistry and Botany.

March 11th, 1858.

MATERIA MEDICA.

1. What is Ipecacuanha? what are its actions? and state the Pharmacopœia preparations, and their doses.

2. What is Opium? what are its physiological effects on man in a full medicinal dose? and what are its uses?

3. State the Pharmacopœia process for the preparation of Tartar Emetic from the Sesqui-sulphuret of Antimony; state its actions, its preparations, and their doses.

4. State the Pharmacopœia process for the preparation of Calomel. What are its actions? what its doses? and what are the ingredients of Plummer's pills.

GEORGE C. M. BIRDWOOD, M.D., Assist. Surgeon,
Acting Professor of Materia Medica.

Saturday, March 13th, 1858.

APPENDIX O.

Report of the Final Examination by the Government Examiner.

To W. 'HART, Esq.,

Secretary to Government, General Department.

SIR,—The Final or Diploma Examinations of the Students of the Grant Medical College having terminated on the 3rd instant, I have the honour to submit, in duplicate, a report of the result, for the information of Government and the Director General of Public Instruction.

2. In conducting the Examinations I have had the able assistance of Drs. Winchester, Glasse, and Woosnam, as Assessors, and of the Acting Principal and Professors of the College.

3. Four Candidates presented themselves, viz. :—

Bhicajee Amroot.
Wamon Wassoodave.
A. P. de Andrade.
Rustomjee Cowasjee.

4. The examinations in Clinical Medicine and Surgery commenced in February, and were conducted daily in the Wards of the Jamsetjee Jejeebhoy Hospital until March.

5. The examinations in Medicine, Surgery, Midwifery, the Diseases of Women and Children, and Medical Jurisprudence, written and oral, were conducted on eight separate days. The questions for the written examinations on these subjects are appended ; and the oral were conducted, as in former years, in the presence of the Assessors, the Acting Principal, and Professors.

6. In Practical Surgery, each Student performed a capital operation and tied a principal artery.

7. In Practical Toxicology, several articles of food, contain-ing poison, were submitted to analysis, and in our presence they were satisfactorily determined.

8. In Midwifery two Candidates failed in their examinations, one also in Medicine, Surgery, and Medical Jurisprudence; and the fourth, on the second day of examination, withdrew his name from the list of competitors, as will be seen from the accompanying Tabular Statement.

9. The final result, therefore, is that none of the Candidates have been pronounced by the Assessors and myself as qualified for the Diploma.

10. This announcement will, no doubt, disappoint the hopes of Government, considering the superior advantages held out by the Grant College for the acquirement of Medical and Surgical knowledge, the high character also stamped upon the College by the rare professional endowments of its late Principal, Dr. Morehead, and the well-known zeal and efficiency of the present Acting Principal and Professors; but, discouraging as it is, it appears to me better for the honour and advancement of the Col-lege, and the interests of the community, that such a result should rather be declared, than that the Assessors and myself should permit the standard of qualification to be, in any degree, lowered.

11. The cause of the present failure is ascribed, and I be-lieve rightly, to defective preliminary education, and to the want of a true taste for the study of Medicine; but, with the powerful agents now at work for the removal of such defects, and the improvement of native education, there is reason to hope that the existing obstacles to the progress and extension of Medical knowledge in India will gradually become less, and the great benefits to be derived from this College be more known and appreciated by the inhabitants of Western India.

I have the honour to be,
Sir,
Your most obedient Servant,

(Signed) W. ARBUCKLE,
Government Examiner.

Result of Diploma Examination.—Session 1857-58.

Names.	Medicine.	Surgery.	Midwifery.	Medical Jurisprudence.	Remarks.
Bhicajee Amroot...............	Qualified.	Qualified.	Not qualified.	Qualified.	Not qualified.
Wamon Wassoodave	Qualified.	Qualified.	Not qualified.	Qualified.	Not qualified.
A. P. de Andrade	Not qualified.	Not qualified.	Qualified.	Not qualified.	Not qualified.
Rustomjee Cowasjee	Not qualified.	Not qualified.	Withdrawn.		

(Signed) W. ARBUCKLE, M.D.,

Government Examiner.

8

DIPLOMA EXAMINATION.

Medicine.

1. What do you understand by Epidemic Cholera? Describe its symptoms, diagnosis from Bilious Cholera, and Irritant Poisoning; the treatment in the different stages of the disease; and the means you would adopt to check its fatal influence when it breaks out in a regiment on the march, or amongst prisoners in a jail.

2. What are the symptoms and course of a case of confluent Small Pox? Mention the diseases with which it may be confounded in its earlier stages, the treatment to be adopted, and the period when the most danger is to be apprehended.

3. State how Dropsy is produced by diseased conditions of the liver, heart, and kidneys : your treatment of Dropsy arising from such causes.

4. Describe what is meant by Anœmic Murmurs, their causes, and how they are to be distinguished from Organic Murmurs. What treatment would you pursue to remove the conditions on which these Anœmic Murmurs depend ?

(Signed) W. Arbuckle, M.D.,
Government Examiner.

March 19th, 1858.

Surgery.

1. What are the symptoms which distinguish concussion from compression of the Brain? State the causes of compression, and the treatment to be adopted in its different forms.

2. Describe the chief difference between Gunshot wounds and other wounds ; the circumstances which would induce you to amputate, and whether you would have recourse to primary or secondary amputation ; and your reasons for the same.

3. Describe the course of an Inguinal Hernia; the symptoms of strangulated Inguinal Hernia; and the treatment to be followed. If an operation be required, describe the method of performing it, and state the dangers to be apprehended from the same.

4. What is the most common disease of the Legs? Describe its symptoms and varieties; and the nature of the operation best suited to each for the improvement of vision.

(Signed)   W. Arbuckle, M.D.,
Government Examiner.

March 20th, 1858.

Midwifery.

1. What are the indications for the use of the short forceps during labour? How are such instruments to be applied and used?

2. Describe the different forms of Puerperal Convulsions, and their treatment.

3. What are the precautions to be observed in administering Chloroform during labour?

4. What are the deciduous Teeth? Describe the usual order of their appearance in the child, and the circumstances under which the use of the gum lancet is indicated.

5. What do you understand by a fibrous tumour of the Uterus? Mention its usual character and situation; how it may be distinguished from an ovarian tumour; and your prognosis and treatment of fibrous tumours of the Uterus.

(Signed)   W. Arbuckle, M.D.,
Government Examiner.

March 27th, 1858.

52

MEDICAL JURISPRUDENCE.

1. You are called to a case of supposed Poisoning by opium : how would you recognise it during life, and determine it after death?

2. A fatal case of Poisoning occurs to you in the Mofussil, and it is desirable to have the chemical investigation conducted by the Chemical Analyst at the Presidency : state how you would proceed.

3. A dead body is found in a well : how would you determine whether the person had been drowned, or put into the well after death ?

4. A dead body of a newly born child is found in a drain, and you are requested by the Magistrate to send him a Medical report of the case : state the important circumstances to be ascertained, and how you would proceed. A woman in the neighbourhood is also suspected to be the mother of the child : state the medical evidence that would induce you to say that such suspicions were well grounded.

(Signed)   W. ARBUCKLE, M.D.,
Government Examiner.

April 3rd, 1858.

Copy of a Resolution, passed by Government under date the 26th *April* 1858.

1. The thanks of Government should be communicated to Dr. Arbuckle, and to the gentlemen who have aided him as Assessors.

2. The Governor in Council feels much disappointed at the result of the late Examinations, but entirely concurs with Dr. Arbuckle in his opinion that the honour and success of the College and the interests of the public alike require that the standard of qualification, hitherto upheld, should be jealously preserved from deterioration.

3. In the observations recorded by Government with respect to the Examinations of March and April·1857, the first of the two obstacles noticed in para. 11 of Dr. Arbuckle's present letter, as interfering with the success of the Grant Medical College, was particularly noticed, and will, doubtless, have received due attention from the Director of Public Instruction. With respect to the second, Government consider that, if the classes of the community for whom this College was first instituted, and to whom it holds out advantages in Medical Education afforded by no similar institution of which they are aware in any part of the world, either decline to avail themselves of it, or are found to be generally incapable of doing credit to the instruction which is given to them, something must be done to extend the advantages of the College Education to others.

4. The Governor in Council is inclined to believe that, could certain disadvantages now attendant on the residence in Bombay of lads not under the immediate control of their parents be alleviated, many British-born and Anglo-Indian Officers, belonging to the higher grades of the uncovenanted Service, as well as Warrant Officers and others, not in a position to send their sons to be educated in England, would be glad to offer them as Candidates for admission to the benefits of an education, which, when complete, would make them members of an honourable profession, and ensure them at an early age a respectable independence in this country or almost any other.

5. To youths of these classes, selected in consideration of their approved talents, sound preliminary education, and general aptitude for the Medical Profession, His Lordship in Council would be glad to see the Grant Medical College made fully available.

6. As a first step towards this, the Director of Public Instruction should be requested to ascertain if any arrangement could be made for lodging and boarding, in an inexpensive but respectable manner, and under the general control and guardianship of some judicious and trustworthy superintendent in the neighbourhood of the Grant College, such European and Anglo-Indian youths as might be selected for admission to it. Mr. Howard should also be requested to ascertain, as far as he can, by means of his Educational Inspectors or otherwise, if the belief expressed above in the 4th para. of this Resolution is likely to prove correct.

7. Copies of the Examiner's Report and of this Resolution should, according to usual custom, be appended to the Annual Report of the Grant Medical College, which will be included in the general Education Report of the Presidency.

(True copy)

(Signed)   E. I. HOWARD,
Director of Public Instruction.

APPENDIX P.

GRANT MEDICAL COLLEGE.

NOTIFICATION.

THE following SCHOLARSHIPS and PRIZES will be OPEN for COMPETITION at the close of the Session 1857-58, viz. in the month of April 1858 :—

I.

To Fourth Year Students, who have qualified for " First Examination Certificates."

A CARNAC Scholarship, of Rs. 25 monthly, for proficiency in conducting the duties of Clinical Clerk, and in knowledge of Practical Medicine and Pathology. The Examination will be conducted in the Clinical Ward and in the Dissecting-room.

An ANDERSON Scholarship, of Rs. 25 monthly, for proficiency in conducting the duties of Surgical Dresser, and in knowledge of Practical Surgery and Surgical Anatomy. The Examination will be conducted in the Clinical Surgical Ward and in the Dissecting-room.

II.

To Third Year Students, who have qualified for " First Examination Certificates."

A REID Scholarship, of Rs. 20 monthly, for proficiency in Anatomy and Physiology. The Examination will be partly conducted in the Dissecting-room.

An ANDERSON Scholarship, of Rs. 15 monthly, for proficiency in the Second Degree in Anatomy and Physiology. The Examination will be partly conducted in the Dissecting-room.

A FARISH Scholarship, of Rs. 20 monthly, for proficiency in Materia Medica and Practical Pharmacy. The Examination will be partly conducted in the Laboratory.

III.

To Second Year Students.

An ANDERSON Scholarship, of Rs. 15 monthly, for proficiency in Anatomy.

A CARNAC Scholarship, of Rs. 15 monthly, for proficiency in Chemistry, Theoretical and Practical.

A FARISH Scholarship, of Rs. 15 monthly, for proficiency in Materia Medica and Practical Pharmacy.

IV.

To First Year Students.

A CARNAC Scholarship, of Rs. 10 monthly, for proficiency in Anatomy.

A FARISH Scholarship, of Rs. 10 monthly, for proficiency in Chemistry.

———

SIR JAMSETJEE JEJEEBHOY's Medical Prize of Rs. 250, open for competition to the Graduates of the Session, will be awarded for proficiency in Operative Surgery.

The McLENAAN Scholarship, of Rs. 25 monthly, with a Silver Prize Medal, open for competition to the Graduates of the Session, will be awarded for great proficiency in the Principles and Practice of Midwifery.

The Examinations for this Prize and Scholarship will be conducted, after the close of the Diploma Examinations, by the Principal and Professors of Medicine, Surgery, and Midwifery, chiefly in the Clinical Ward of the Hospital, and in the Dissecting-room.

Graduates desirous of competing are required to intimate their intention to the Principal of the College after the termination of the Diploma Examination.

(Signed) C. MOREHEAD,
Principal Grant Medical College.

Bombay, Grant Medical College,
10th November 1857.

E. I. HOWARD,
Director of Public Instruction.

APPENDIX Q.

Scholarships awarded to the Students of the Grant Medical College, at the close of the Session 1857-58.

CARNAC SCHOLARSHIP, of Rs. 25 monthly, for proficiency in conducting the duties of Clinical Clerk, and in knowledge of Practical Medicine and Pathology, open to Fourth Year Students who have qualified for " First Examination Certificate," has been awarded to *Burjorjee Framjee.*

2. ANDERSON SCHOLARSHIP, of Rs. 25 monthly, for proficiency in conducting the duties of Surgical Dresser, and in knowledge of Practical Surgery and Surgical Anatomy, open to Fourth Year Students who have qualified for " First Examination Certificate," has been awarded to *Eduljee Nusserwanjee.*

3. REID SCHOLARSHIP, of Rs. 20 monthly, for proficiency in Anatomy and Physiology, open to Third Year Students who have qualified for " First Examination Certificate," has been awarded to *J. N. Mendonça.*

4. ANDERSON SCHOLARSHIP, of Rs. 15 monthly, for proficiency in the second degree in Anatomy and Physiology, open to Third Year Students who have qualified for " First Examination Certificate," has been awarded to *Surfoodin Sumsoodin.*

5. FARISH SCHOLARSHIP, of Rs. 20 monthly, for proficiency in Materia Medica and Practical Pharmacy, open to Third Year Students who have qualified for " First Examination Certificate," has been awarded to *Muncherjee Byramjee.*

6. ANDERSON SCHOLARSHIP, of Rs. 15 monthly, for proficiency in Anatomy, open to Second Year Students, to *Nusserwanjee Dhunjeebhoy ;* but as Nusserwanjee Dhunjeebhoy is the successful competitor for the Farish Scholarship, the pecuniary

9

advantage of this Scholarship will pass to the next in proficiency, *Dorabjee Hormusjee.*

7. CARNAC SCHOLARSHIP, of Rs. 15 monthly, for proficiency in Chemistry, Theoretical and Practical, open to Second Year Students, has been awarded to *Furdoonjee Byramjee.*

8. FARISH SCHOLARSHIP, of Rs. 15 monthly, for proficiency in Materia Medica and Practical Pharmacy, open to Second Year Students, has been awarded to *Nusserwanjee Dhunjeebhoy.*

9. CARNAC SCHOLARSHIP, of Rs. 10 monthly, for proficiency in Anatomy, open to First Year Students, has been awarded to *Shantaram Wittul.*

10. FARISH SCHOLARSHIP, of Rs. 10 monthly, for proficiency in Chemistry, open to First Year Students, has been awarded to *Kaikusrao Rustomjee.*

11. THE SIR JAMSETJEE JEJEEBHOY MEDICAL PRIZE, and the McLENNAN SCHOLARSHIP of Rs. 25 monthly, with silver prize Medal for great proficiency in Operative Surgery and in the Principles and Practice of Midwifery, open to the Graduates of the Session, have not been awarded, as no Diploma has this year been conferred.

HERBERT GIRAUD,
Acting Principal, Grant Medical College.

APPENDIX R.

Written Questions in Anatomy, Chemistry, and Physiology, to First and Second Year Students; and in Medicine and Surgery, to Third and Fourth Year Students.

FIRST AND SECOND YEAR STUDENTS.

Anatomy.

1. Describe all the Ligaments that connect the Dorsal Vertebræ to each other.
2. Describe the Diaphragm.
3. Describe the Ligaments of the Liver.
4. Describe the Axis.

Physiology.

1. Describe the composition of healthy Urine.
2. Describe the Physiology of the fifth pair of Cranial Nerves.
3. Describe the Mucous Membrane of the Tongue, and state what is known of the function of each part of the Mucous Membrane.

(Signed)   T. M. LOWNDS, M.D.,
Professor of Anatomy and Physiology.

FIRST AND SECOND YEAR STUDENTS.

Chemistry.

1. Explain the conditions under which the three forms of Matter (*solid, liquid, and gaseous*) exist.
2. Explain the phenomena of the Electrical Machine.
3. The properties, chemical relations, and uses of Lime.
4. Explain the phenomena of Alcoholic Fermentation.

HERBERT GIRAUD, M.D.,
Professor of Chemistry and Botany.

March 11th, 1858.

60

THIRD AND FOURTH YEAR STUDENTS.

Medicine.

1. Give the conditions of system under which active and passive Congestions arise.

2. Describe the state of system in which general Dropsy may be produced without organic disease.

3. Describe what you mean by the term Intermittent Fever. State the varieties, and how they are distinguished. Give the symptoms of a case of Quotidian Intermittent Fever complicated with Bronchitis, and its prognosis.

4. Describe the course of Variola. State what you mean by the term Modified Small-pox, and how it differs from ordinary Variola ; and state the modes in which death is produced in Variola, and at what period of the disease it usually takes place in fatal cases.

March 19*th*, 1858.

T. M. LOWNDS, M.D.,
Officiating Professor of Medicine.

THIRD YEAR STUDENTS.

Surgery.

1. What is the nature of the processes of Ulceration and Mortification ? Describe the local signs of Gangrene.

2. What are the peculiarities of Erysipelatous inflammations ? Describe the symptoms and treatment of Cutaneous Erysipelas.

3. Describe the process of Union of Fractured Bones.

FOURTH YEAR STUDENTS.

1. Describe the diseases of the Coats of Arteries, and state the secondary affections which occasionally result.

2. What are the symptoms of Strangulated Hernia ? Describe generally the treatment to be adopted.

3. Enumerate the various operations for Evacuating the Bladder in Retention of Urine, and state the cases to which they are respectively applicable.

March 19*th*, 1858.

G. R. BALLINGALL,
Professor of Surgery.

APPENDIX S.

Result of Examination of First Year Students.
Session 1857-58.

No.	Names.	Anato-my.	Chemis-try.	Practical Phar-macy.	Total.*
1	Shantaram Wittul........	8	8	5	21
2	Kaikusrao Rustomjee	7	8	5	20
3	Burjorjee Byramjee	7	7	5	19
4 {	Framjee Bomanjee	5	7	5	17
	Nusserwanjee Jehangeerjee .	6	6	5	17

* The highest number marks the greatest merit. Ten has been taken as the standard of excellence in each subject.

HERBERT GIRAUD,
Acting Principal, Grant Medical College.

Result of Examination of Second Year Students.—Session 1857-58.

No.	Names.	Anatomy.	Physiology.	Chemistry.	Materia Medica.	Botany.	Practical Chemistry and Pharmacy.	Total.*	Remarks.
1	Nusserwanjee Dhunjeebhoy.	9	6	7	9	9	Good.	40	
2	Furdoonjee Byramjee......	7	4	9	7	8	Good.	35	
3	Dorabjee Hormusjee	9	6	6	4	7	Good.	32	
3	Abdool Kurrim Lukmonjee.	8	4	7	6	7	Good.	32	
4	Ambaram Kavalram	7	5	7	4	6	Good.	20	
5	Framjee Shapoorjee	5	3	8	4	7	Good.	27	
6	Pestonjee Nowrojee........	3	3	5	4	3	Indifferent.	18	
7	Nanabhoy Eduljee	4	2	5	4	2	Bad.	17	
8	P. A. de Nazareth	4	3	5	1	1	Good.	14	
9	Hurreechund Gopall	3	0	3	2	2	Good.	10	
10	Soonderrow Bhaskerjee	2	0	2	1	1	Bad.	6	
11	Hormusjee Pestonjee	3	1	0	0	0	Bad.	4	

* The highest number marks the greatest merit. Ten has been taken as the standard of excellence in each subject.

HERBERT GIRAUD,
Acting Principal, Grant Medical College.

Result of Examination of Third Year Students.—Session 1857-58.

No.	Names.	Medicine.	Surgery.	Total.*	Remarks.
1 {	Muncherjee Byramjee	7	7	14	
	Byramjee Nowrojee	7	7	14	
2	J. N. Mendonça	6	6	12	
3	Dossabhoy Pestonjee	7	4	11	
4	Surfoodin Sumsoodin	3	6	9	
5	Cowasjee Hormusjee	3	5	8	
6 {	Heerajee Eduljee	3	4	7	
	Dadabhoy Jamasjee	3	4	7	
7	Rustomjee Hormusjee	Absent.	Absent.		
8	Jamsetjee Byramjee	Absent.	Absent.		
9	Cowasjee Mendozjee	Absent.	Absent.		

* The highest number marks the greatest merit. Ten has been taken as the standard of excellence in each subject.

HERBERT GIRAUD,

Acting Principal, Grant Medical College.

Result of Examination of Fourth Year Students.—Session 1857-58.

No.	Names.	Medicine.	Surgery.	Midwifery.	Medical Jurisprudence.	Total. *	Remarks.
1	Eduljee Nusserwanjee	8	8	10	5	31	
2	Manockjee Aderjee	6	6	7	8	27	
3	Burjorjee Framjee............	7	8	5	5	25	
4	Pestonjee Bomanjee	5	6	8	4	23	
5	Jejeebhoy Bazonjee	6	5	4	4	19	
6	Huree Vishnoo......:.........	4	4	1	2	11	
7	Ramchundra Narayen	Absent.	Absent.	Absent.	Absent.		
8	Pestonjee Muncherjee	Absent.	Absent.	Absent.	Absent.		

* The highest number marks the greatest merit. Ten has been taken as the standard of excellence in each subject.

HERBERT GIRAUD,
Acting Principal, Grant Medical College.

APPENDIX T.

Abstract of Sums paid to the Students of the Grant Medical College, on account of the Sir Jamsetjee Jejeebhoy Book Fund, for the Year 1856-57.

Names.	Amount.		
	Rs.	a.	p.
Bhikajee Amroot	15	8	0
Wamon Wassoodave	6	12	0
A. P. de Andrade	6	14	0
Jumnadas Hurgovindas	12	4	0
Rustomjee Cowasjee	11	5	0
Eduljee Nusserwanjee	22	4	3
Burjorjee Framjee	19	4	0
Pestonjee Bomanjee	23	9	6
Ramchundra Narrayen	12	7	0
Manockjee Aderjee	18	8	0
Huree Vishnoo	11	11	0
Pestonjee Muncherjee	18	13	0
Jejeebhoy Bazonjee	21	7	0
Muncherjee Byramjee	10	12	6
J. N. Mendonça	12	2	0
Byramjee Naorosjee	7	6	0
Surfoodin Sumsoodin	10	1	0
Dossabhoy Pestonjee	3	0	0
Rustomjee Hormusjee	3	13	0
Dadabhoy Jamasjee	1	12	0
Cowasjee Mendozjee	5	9	6
Cowasjee Hormusjee	8	10	0
Furdoonjee Byramjee	18	6	0
Ambaram Kavalram	11	12	0

10

Names.	Amount.		
	Rs.	a.	p.
Nusserwanjee Dhunjeebhoy.....................	12	4	0
Dorabjee Hormusjee	12	9	0
Framjee Shapoorjee............................	13	12	0
P. A. de Nazareth	11	6	0
Abdool Kurrim Luckmonjee	11	13	0
Hurreechund Gopal...........................	16	10	0
Nanabhoy Eduljee	14	4	6
Soonderrow Bhaskerjee	9	7	0
Pestonjee Nowrojee	11	5	0
Hormusjee Pestonjee	12	0	0
Aid in purchasing the Jamsetjee Jejeebhoy Hospital Formula to the Student ....t.	11	0	0
Total.... Rupees	430	5	3

(Signed) C. MOREHEAD,

Principal, Grant Medical College.

APPENDIX U.

Rules regarding Text-Books.

1. Students are to provide themselves with the Text-Books fixed for the different Classes, before or during the first week of the Session.

2. Bills for books purchased by Students are to be shown, with the books, to the Professor of the subject to which the books relate, within a month after payment. The Professor will affix his initials to the bill, and no bill without the initials of a Professor will be considered, at the end of the Session, to have a claim on the Jamsetjee Jejeebhoy Book Fund.

3. The income of the Jamsetjee Jejeebhoy Book Fund will be disbursed exclusively in aid of the purchase of the fixed Text-Books, and in occasional additions to the Students' collection of books of reference.

4. Aid from the Jamsetjee Jejeebhoy Fund will not be granted to any Student unless he exhibits, on each occasion of application, his complete series of the Class Books on the subjects he has studied and is studying.

5. The bills of regular booksellers will alone be acknowledged.

LIST OF TEXT-BOOKS.

The following are the Text-Books in use, and Students in purchasing them should be careful to obtain the latest editions:—

Chemistry.

Fownes' Manual of Chemistry.
Odling's Practical Chemistry.

68.

Anatomy.
Elements of Anatomy, by Jones Quain, M.D.
Demonstrations of Anatomy, by George Viner Ellis.

Physiology.
Hand-Book of Physiology, by William Senhouse Kirkes, M.D.

Materia Medica.
Christison's Dispensatory.

Botany.
Balfour's Outlines of Botany.

Medicine.
Watson's Lectures on the Practice of Physic.
Pathological Anatomy, by Jones and Sievking.

Surgery.
Science and Art of Surgery, by Erichsen.
Jones' Ophthalmic Medicine and Surgery.

Medical Jurisprudence.
Guy's Forensic Medicine.

Midwifery.
Murphy's Lectures on Midwifery.
West on Diseases of. Children.

C. MOREHEAD,
Principal, Grant Medical College.

November, 1857.

APPENDIX V.

STUDENTS.

Rules regarding Absence from Roll-calls.

1. Every Student not present at a Roll-call will, for the time, be marked "absent."

2. Students unable to attend from sickness must furnish a certificate to that effect, according to a fixed form, signed, in the event of the sickness exceeding two days, by a qualified Medical Practitioner, and for the shorter period by a qualified Medical Practitioner or the father or guardian of the Student. Printed copies of the certificate will be supplied by the College Clerk.

3. Students absenting themselves on days not recognised by the College as holidays, are required to furnish a certificate, according to a fixed form, that the absence was unavoidable, signed by some person of acknowledged respectability. Printed copies of the certificate will be supplied by the College Clerk. Students absent under this rule more than eight days in the course of the Session will not be allowed to compete for Scholarships.

4. The record of attendance of each Student will be made at the close of each month.

The Rules which follow, regarding absence, are exclusive of absence on recognised holidays, from sickness duly certified, and on unavoidable grounds.

5. Students who have not been absent at more than five Roll-calls during the Session are entitled to a certificate of having attended "very regularly."

6. Those who have not been absent at more than 15 Roll-calls are entitled to a certificate of having attended "regularly."

7. Those who have been absent at more than 15, but not more than 25 Roll-calls, shall be certified as having attended "not regularly."

8. Those absent at more than 25 Roll-calls shall be certified as having attended "irregularly."

9. Those absent at more than 40 Roll-calls as having attended "very irregularly."

A copy of the certificate of attendance thus granted annually to each student will be recorded in the books of the College.

C. MOREHEAD,
Principal, Grant Medical College.

Bombay, June 1857.

APPENDIX W.

STUDENT APPRENTICES.

Rules regarding Absence from Roll-Calls.

1. Every Student Apprentice not present at a Roll-call will, for the time, be marked " absent."

2. The Apothecary of the J; J. Hospital will send every morning, at 10 A. M., to the College Clerk, a list of the Student Apprentices who are sick in quarters ; also, at other periods in the course of the day, a memorandum of the names of those who may have reported themselves sick after 10 o'clock ; and the hour at which the Report was made will be entered in the memorandum. The plea of sickness will be admitted only in respect to Student Apprentices reported as above.

3. The only Officers authorised to grant private leave of absence from the College Roll-calls, are the Principal of the College and the Surgeon of the J. J. Hospital. Printed copies of the " Leave Ticket" will be supplied by the College Clerk ; and no Student Apprentice is to absent himself on leave till he has obtained the necessary ticket, duly signed by one of the authorised Officers.

4. The record of attendance of each Student Apprentice will be made at the close of each month, and " absent" entered opposite to each name so recorded in the Roll-calls and not accounted for by Sick Report or Private Leave Ticket.

5. Student Apprentices absent without leave from 1, 2, 3, 4 Roll-calls in the month, will forfeit, during the subsequent month, money compensation for rations for one, two, three, or four weeks respectively.

6. Student Apprentices absent without leave from 10 Roll-calls in the course of the Session will be disqualified for competition for the Burnes and McLennan Medals and other Prizes.

C. MOREHEAD,
Principal, Grant Medical College.

Bombay, October 1857.

APPENDIX X.

*List of Books purchased on account of Mr. Willoughby's
Prize for Students' Collection of Books of Reference.*

Copies.

1. Todd and Bowman's Physiological Anatomy.
1. Pereira's Materia Medica.
1. Miller's Elements of Chemistry.
2. Balfour's Class-book of Botany.
1. Lindley's Vegetable Kingdom.
2. Williams' Principles of Medicine.
2. Morehead's Clinical Researches.
2. Budd, on Diseases of the Liver.
1. Paget's Surgical Pathology.
1. Lionel Beale's work on the Microscope.
1. Taylor, on Poisons.
2. Bird, on Urinary Deposits.

HERBERT GIRAUD,
Acting Principal, Grant Medical College.

APPENDIX Y.

DONATIONS TO THE LIBRARY.

From C. Morehead, Esq., M.D.

The Cyclopædia, or Universal Dictionary of Arts, Sciences, and
Literature, by A. Rees, Esq., with Plates.   45 vols.

Dictionary of the English Language, by S. Johnson, Esq. 2 vols.

Edinburgh Medical and Physical Dictionary.   2 vols.

Treatise of the Materia Medica, by W. Cullen, M.D.   2 vols.

Latin Vocabulary.

Description and Treatment of Cutaneous Diseases; Order I.
Papulous Eruptions, by R. William, M.D.

A System of Materia Medica and Pharmacy, by J. Murray,
M.D.

Elements of Natural Philosophy, by G. Bird, M.D.

On the Use and Abuse of Alcoholic Liquors in Health and
Disease, by W. B. Carpenter, Esq.

A System of Phrenology, by G. Combe, Esq.   2 vols.

A Treatise on Fever, by S. Smith, Esq.

A Manual of Comparative Anatomy; Translated from the German
of J. F. Blumenbach, by W. Lawrence, Esq.

Traité de l'Inflammation, by J. Thomson, Esq.

Exposition des Principes de la Nouvelle Doctrine Médicale, by J.
M. Goupil, Esq.

Elémens d'Hygiène, by E. Tourlell, Esq.   2 vols,

Rapports du Physique et du Moral de l'Homme, by P. J. G.
Cabanis, Esq.   2 vols.

Traité d'Anatomic, by H. Cloquet, Esq.   2 vols.

Celsus, de Medicina, c. N. variorum.

11

Celsus, de Medicina, Edinburgh.

Dictionnaire des Sciences Médicales. 15 vols.

Dictionnaire de Medicine, in 21 vols., but 13th vol. wanting.

Traité d'Anatomie Chirurgicale, by A. S. Velpeau. 2 vols.

Maladies de la Peau, by H. E. Sepedel, Esq.

Traité de Geognosie, by J. F. d'Anbinson, Esq.

Elemens d'Anatomie Générale, ou Description de tous les Genres d'Organes qui composent le Corps Humain, by P. A. Béclard, Esq.

Manuel d'Ornithologie, ou Description des Genres et des Principales Espèces d'Oiseaux, by R. P. Lesson, Esq.

Manuel d'Entomologie, ou Histoire Naturelle des Insects, by Boilard, Esq. 2 vols.

Manuel de Mammalogie, ou Histoire Naturelle des Mammifères, by R. P. Lesson, Esq.

Manuel d'Astronomie, ou Traité Elémentaire de cette Science, by M. Bailly, Esq.

From Dr. Beatty.

Observations on the Surgical Pathology of the Larynx and Trachea, by W. H. Porter, A.M.

Clinical Lectures on Venereal Diseases, by Richard Carmichael, M.R.I.A.

Practical Remarks on the Treatment of Aneurism by Compression, by J. Tufnell, M.R.I.A.

A Treatise on Fractures in the Vicinity of Joints, and on certain Forms of Accidental and Congenital Dislocation, by R. W. Smith, M.D., M.R.I.A.

Practical Observations on the Venereal Disease, and on the Use of Mercury, by A. Colles, M.D.

On Indigestion, and certain Bilious Disorders often conjoined with it, to which are added Short Notes on Diet, by G. C. Child, M.D.

From Dr. Downes.

Pathological and Surgical Observations on the Diseases of the Joints, by B. C. Brodie, F.R.S.

Practical Observations in Surgery, by H. Earle, F.R.S.

Lectures on the Blood, and on the Anatomy, Physiology, and Surgical Pathology of the Vascular System of the Human Body, by J. Wilson, F.R.S.

Principles of Military Surgery, comprising Observations on the Arrangement, Police, and Practice of Hospitals, by J. Hennan, M.D., F.R.S.E.

On Diagnosis, by Marshall Hall, M.D.

Practical Synopsis of Cutaneous Diseases, by T. Bateman, M.D., F.R.S.

Treatise on the Venereal Disease, by J. Hunter, Esq.

Treatise on Symptomatic Fevers, including Inflammations, Hæmorrhages, and Mucous Discharges, by A. P. W. Philip, M.D., F.R.S.E.

Elements of the Theory and Practice of Physic, designed for the Use of Students, by G. Gregory, M.D.

Elémens d'Anatomie Générale, ou Description de tous les Genres d'Organes, par by P. A. Béclard d'Angers.

Treatise on Ruptures, containing an Anatomical Description of each Species, with an Account of its Symptoms, Progress, and Treatment, by W. Lawrence, F.R.S.

An Experimental Inquiry into the Law of the Vital Functions, with some Observations on the Nature and Treatment of Internal Diseases, by A. P. W. Philip, M.D., F.R.S.E.

Treatise on Fevers, including the various Species of Simple and Eruptive Fevers, by A. P. W. Philip, M.D., F.R.S.E.

The Influence of Tropical Climates on European Constitutions, being a Treatise on the Principal Diseases incidental to Europeans in the East and West Indies, Mediterranean, and Coast of Africa, by J. Johnson, M.D.

Principles of Surgery for the Use of Chirurgical Students, by J. Pearson, F.R.S.

Treatise on Indigestion and its Consequences, called Nervous and Bilious Complaints, and the Organic Diseases in which they sometimes terminate, by A. P. W. Philip, M.D., F.R.S.E.

Treatise on the Diseases of Arteries and Veins, by J. Hodgson, Esq.

A Synopsis of the Various Kinds of Difficult Parturition, with Practical Remarks on the Management of Labours, by S. Merriman, M.D., F.L.S.

Treatise on the Diseases of the Chest, by — Laenneck, Esq.

Works of Mallhen Baillie, M.D., to which is prefixed an Account of his Life collected from authentic sources, by J. Wardrop. 2 vols.

Treatise on the Blood, Inflammation, and Gunshot Wounds, by J. Hunter, Esq. 2 vols.

Surgical Works, by J. Abernethy, F.R.S. 3 vols.

A Practical Work on the Diseases of the Eye and their Treatment Medically, Topically, and by Operation, by F. Tyrrell. 2 vols.

Treatise on Poison, by R. Christison, M.D.

Medico-Chirurgical Transactions. 4 vols. 2nd edition.

Medico-Chirurgical Transactions. 5 vols. from 1809 to 1814.

The Chirurgical Works of Percivall Potts, F.R.S.; to which are added a Short Account of the Life of the Author, a Method of Curing the Hydrocele by Injection, and occasional Notes and Observations, by Sir J. Earle, F.R.S. 3 vols.

From the Geographical Society of Bombay.

No. 13 of their Transactions—

From Pathological Society of London.

No. 8 of their Transactions.

From M. Thompson, Esq.

Principles and Practice of Obstetric Medicine, in a Series of Systematic Dissertations on Midwifery and on the Diseases of Women and Children, illustrated by numerous Plates, by David D. Davis, M.D., M.R.S.L. 2 vols.

From Mr. Burjorjee Dorabjee, Graduate of the College.

Practical Treatise on Inflammation of the Uterus, by J. H. Bennet, M.D.

A Course of Lectures on Dental Physiology and Surgery, by
J. Tomes, Esq.

A Treatise on Dislocations and Fractures of the Joints, by Sir
* A. Cooper, Bart., F.R.S.

Chemistry of Organic Bodies and Vegetables, by T. Thomson,
M.D.

Practical Treatise on the Diseases of Children and Infants at the
Breast, translated from the French of M. Bouchat; with
Notes and Additions, by P. H. Bird, F.R.C.S.

Science and Art of Surgery, by J. Erichsen, Esq.

Chelius's System of Surgery, by J. F. South, Esq.   2 vols.

Practical Pharmacy, by F. Mohr, P.D., and T. Redwood, Esq.

The Modern Treatment of Syphilitic Diseases, both Primary and
Secondary, by L. Parker, Esq.

A Practical Treatise on the Management and Diseases of Children, by R. T. Evanson, M.D., and H. Maunsell, M.D.

A Practical Treatise on the Diseases of Children, by J. M. Coley,
M.D.

Lectures on the Diseases of Infancy and Childhood, by C. West,
* M.D.

On the Nature and Treatment of Stomach and Renal Diseases,
by W. Prout, M.D., F.R.S.

An Introduction to Botany, by J. Lindley, P.D., F.R.S. 2 vols.

Outlines of Pathology and Practice of Medicine, by W. P. Ali-
son, Esq.

Element of Chemical Analysis, Qualitative and Quantitative, by
E. A. Parnell, Esq.

Principles of Medicine, comprising general Pathology and Therapeutics, by C. J. B. Williams, M.D., F.R.S.

On Diseases of the Liver, by G. Budd, M.D., F.R.S.

Lectures on the Principles and Practice of Surgery, by B. B.
Cooper, F.R.S.

The Principles of Midwifery, by J. Burns, F.R.S.

Medical Gazette (vols. 1 to 8), from December 1827 to September 1831.

Elements of Chemistry, by A. Fyfe, M.D., F.R.S.E.

The Lancet (vols. 1 and 2) for 1840-1841.

Lectures on Diseases of the Eye, by J. Morgan, F.L.S.

Lectures on Anatomy, Surgery, and Pathology, including Observations on the Nature and Treatment of Local Diseases, by J. Abernethy, Esq., F.R.S.

Institutes of Surgery, by Sir C. Bell, K.G.H. 2 vols.

Elements of the Theory and Practice of Medicine, by G. Gregory, M.D.

A System of Practical Surgery, by J. Lizars, Esq.

Homœopathic Medical Doctrine of " Organon of the Healing Art," by C. H. Devrient, Esq., with Notes by S. Stratten, Esq., M.D.

Clinical Instructions on the more important Diseases of Bengal, by W. Twining, Esq. 2 vols.

The Vegetable Kingdom, or the Structure, Classification, and Uses of Plants, by J. Lindley, P.D., F.R.S., and L.S.

Treatise on Poisons, by R. Christison, M.D., F.R.S.E.

Principles of Surgery, by J. Miller, F.R.S.E.

Elements of Surgery, by R. Liston, Esq.

Practical Surgery, by R. Liston, Esq.

Dr. Underwood's Treatise on the Diseases of Children, edited, with Additions, by H. Davis, M.D.

On the Analysis of the Blood and Urine in Health and Disease, and Treatment of Urinary Diseases, by G. O. Rees, M.D., F.R.S.

The Life of Edward Jenner, M.D., with Illustrations of his Doctrine and Selections from his Correspondence, by J. Baron, M.D., F.R.S. 2 vols.

Transactions of the Medical and Physical Society of Bombay, No. 3.

Report on Small Pox in Calcutta, from 1827 to 1844, by D. Stewart, M.D.

An Essay on Morbid Sensibility of the Stomach and Bowels, by J. Johnson, M.D.

Practical Treatise on Medical Jurisprudence, with so much of Anatomy, Physiology, and the Practice of Medicine and Surgery, by J. Chitty, Esq. Part I.

Cyclopædia of Practice of Medicine. 4 vols.

Cyclopædia of Anatomy and Physiology. 2 vols.

A Theoretical and Practical Treatise on the Diseases of the Skin, by P. Rayer, M.D.

A Dictionary of Practical Surgery, by S. Cooper, Esq.

Medical Bibliography (A and B), by J. Atkinson, Esq.

Principles and Practice of Obstetric Medicine and Surgery, by F. H. Ramsbotham, M.D.

A Compendium of Human and Comparative Pathological Anatomy, by A. W. Otts, M.D.

Pathological and Practical Researches on Diseases of the Stomach, the Intestinal Canal, and the Liver, by J. Abercrombie, M.D.

Pathological and Practical Researches on Diseases of the Brain and the Spinal Cord, by J. Abercrombie, M.D.

•A Treatise on the Functional and Structural Changes of the Liver, by W. E. E. Conwell, M.R.I.A.

Surgical Essay, the Result of Clinical Observations made at Guy's Hospital, by B. B. Cooper, F.R.S.

Constitutional Irritation, and the Pathology of the Nervous System, by B. Travers, F.R.S.

The Principles of Forensic Medicine, by J. G. Smith, M.D.

Animal Chemistry, by J. Liebig, M.D., P.D., F.R.S.

A Treatise on the Structure, Economy, and Diseases of the Ear, by G. Pilcher, Esq.

An Experimental Inquiry into the Laws of the Vital Functions, by A. P. W. Philip, M.D., F.R.S.

A System of Practical Surgery, by J. Lizars, Esq.

The Bengal Pharmacopœia, by W. B. O'Shaughnessy, M.D., F.R.S.

History of Chronic Phlegmasia, by F. J. V. Broussais, M.D. 2 vols.

A Practical Treatise on Uterine Hæmorrhage in connection with Pregnancy and Parturition, by J. Ingleby, Esq.

The Stomach in its Morbid State, by L. Parker, Esq.

A Practical Synopsis of Cutaneous Diseases, by T. Bateman, M.D., F.L.S.

A Discourse on the Phenomena of Sensation, by J. Johnstone, M.D.

Discourses on the Nature and Cure of Wounds, by J. Bell, Surgeon.

Principles of Medicine, by A. Billing, M.D., A.M.

Outlines of General Pathology, by G. Freckleton, M.D., Cantab.

The Nervous System and its Functions, by H. Mayo, F.R.S.

The Principles of Gothic Ecclesiastical Architecture, by M. H. Bloxam, Esq.

Lectures on the Principles and Practice of Midwifery, by J. Blundell, M.D., edited by C. Severn, M.D.

Outlines of Organic Chemistry, by W. Gregory, M.D.

Outlines of Inorganic Chemistry, by W. Gregory, M.D.

The Principles of Surgery, by J. Bell, Esq. 4 vols.

Gradus ad Parnassum, sive Synonymorum et Epithetorum Thesaurus.

Literal Interlineal Translation of the first twenty-three Chapters of Gregory's Conspectus Medicinæ, by R. Venables, A.M.,M.B.

Cholera, Dysentery, and Fever, Pathologically and Practically considered, by C. Searle, M.D.

Year-Book of Facts in Science and Art, for the years 1839 to 1842.

Varicose Veins and Varicose Ulcers, by T. W. Nunn, Esq.

Outlines of Pathological Semeiology, translated from the German of Professor Schill, with copious Notes, by D. Spillan, M.D., A.M.

A short Treatise on Operative Surgery, by C. Averile, Esq.

The Philosophy of Death, or a General Medical and Statistical Treatise on the Nature and Causes of Human Mortality, by J. Reid, Esq.

The Anatomist's Manual, or a Treatise on the Manner of performing all the Parts of Anatomy, by J. P. Maygrier, M.D.P.

Observations on the Extraction of Teeth, with Plates, by J. C. Clendon, Esq. F.R.S.

School Botany, by J. Lindley, Ph.D., F.R.S.

Outlines of Mineralogy and Geology.

History of Freemasonry, from the year 1829 to the present time, by the Rev. G. Oliver, D.D.

New Descriptive Catalogue of Minerals, by J. Mawe, Esq.
Manual for Students who are preparing for Examination at
Apothecaries' Hall, by J. Steggall, M.D.
The Surgeon's Vade-Mecum, by R. Druitt, Esq.
Practical Treatise on the Use of the Blow-Pipe in Chemical and
Animal Analysis, by J. Griffin, Esq.
Clinical Midwifery, by R. Lee, M.D., F.R.S.
Meckel's Manual of Descriptive Pathological Anatomy. 2
vols..
The Surgical Anatomy of the Arteries of the Human Body,
by R. Harrison, M.D.
Management of the Organs of Digestion in Health and in
● Disease, by H. Mayo, Esq., F.R.S.
Treatise on Physiology and Phrenology, by P. M. Roget, M.D.
2 vols.
Practical Essay on some of the Principal Surgical Diseases of
India, by F. II. Brett, Esq., M.R.C.S.L.
The Library of Medicine, by A. Tweedie, M.D., F.R.S. 6 vols.
A Guide to the Practical Study of Diseases of the Eye, by J.
Dixon, Esq.
The Physical Diagnosis of Diseases of the Abdomen, by E. Bal-
lord, M.D.
The Surgical Anatomy of the Groin, the Femoral and Popliteal
Regions, by T. Morton, Esq.
Clinical Introduction to the Practice of Auscultation, by H. M.
Hughes, M.D.
Manual of Pathology, containing the Symptoms, Diagnosis,
and Morbid Characters of Disease, by L. Martinet, D.M.P.,
translated by J. Quain, M.D.
Manual of Therapeutics, by L. Martinet, D.M.P., translated
by R. Norton, M.D., M.R.C.S.
Bedside Manual of Physical Diagnosis, by C. Cowar.
Byron's Works, vols. ii. and iv.
The Life of Sir Isaac Newton, by D. Brewster, LL.D., F.R.S.
An Elementary Introduction to Mineralogy, by W. Phillips, Esq.
Lectures on the Principles and Practice of Midwifery, by E. W.
Murphy, A.M., M.D.

A Synopsis of the various kinds of Difficult Parturition, with Practical Remarks on the Management of Labour, by S. Merriman, M.D., F.L.S.

The Life of Sir Astley Cooper, Bart. 2 vols.

Pathological and Surgical Observations on the Diseases of the Joints, by B. C. Brodie, V.P.R.S.

On the Diseases of Females, by T. J. Graham, M.D.

An Exposition of the Natural System of the Nerves of the Human Body, by C. Bell, Esq.

Sketches of the most prevalent Diseases of India, by J. Annesley, Esq.

Lectures concerning the Diseases of the Urethra, by C. Bell, Esq.

Tables in Illustration of the Theory of Definite Proportionals, showing the Prime Equivalent Numbers of the Elementary Substances, by W. T. Brande, Esq.

Outlines of Geology, by W. T. Brande, Esq.

A Fragment on Government, by J. Bentham, Esq.

The Practice of Medicine, according to the Principles of the Physiological Doctrine, by J. Coster, M.D.

The Practice of Surgery, by J. Miller, F.R.S.E.

A System of Practical Surgery, by W. Fergusson, F.R.S.E.

Manual of Diseases of the Skin, from the French of M.M. Gajenave and Schedel; with Notes and Additions, by T. H. Burgess, M.D.

Lectures on the Principles and Practice of Surgery, by Sir A. Cooper, Bart., F.R.S.

On the Theory and Practice of Midwifery, by E. Churchill, M.D., M.R.I.A.

Dr. Grieve's Translation of Celsus, edited, with Notes, by G. Futvoye, Esq.

The Cabinet Cyclopædia, conducted by the Rev. D. Lardner, LL.D., F.R.S.

Surgical Observations on Tumours, with Cases and Operations, by J. C. Warren, M.D.

HERBERT GIRAUD,
Acting Principal, Grant Medical College.

APPENDIX Z.

Contributions to the Grant Medical College Museum for the Session 1857-58.

From Dr. Morehead.

Specimen of diseased intestine.
*Do. do. heart.

From Dr. Leith.

Specimen of gangrenous liver.

From C. C. Mead, Esq.

Hydatid cyst from peritoneum.

From Dr. Ballingall.

Specimen of diseased intestine.
Do. do. do.
Kidney, with calculus and cyst.
Specimen of antero-posterior curvature.

From J. Kearney, Esq.

Aneurism of ascending aorta.

From Burjorjee Ardaseer, Graduate. G. M. C.

Very large tiger's skull.
Two small ditto.
Frontal bone of black buck.
Humerus of vulture, showing re-united fracture.

Large water-snake, from Sind, preserved in spirits.
Two small snakes, in spirits.
A preserved lizard.
A preserved tænia.
Hypertrophied scrotum, in spirits.
Fatty tumour, in spirits.
Eye, preserved in spirits.

From the Assistant Apothecary, Shaik Cassim.

A portion of necrosed bones.

From Dr. Lownds.

Diseased heart.
Portion of diaphragm, separating distinct abscesses in liver and
lung.
Cancer of liver.
Specimen of diseased lung.
Do.   abnormal origin of vertebral artery.
Do.   diseased knee-joint.
Do.   abscess of pancreas.

T. M. Lownds, M.D.,
Curator of Museum.

APPENDIX AA.

Proceedings of the Grant College Medical Society,
during the Session 1857-58.

Minutes of a Meeting of the Grant College Medical Society, held in the College Library, on Saturday, 11th July 1857, at half-past four P. M.

PRESENT.

Dr. R. Haines........ *Vice-President, in the Chair.*
Mr. S. A. de Carvalho.. *Vice-President.*

Members.

Dr. H. Giraud ; Dr. Rustomjee Byramjee ; Mr. P. F. Gomes ; Mr. J. C. Lisboa ; Mr. Muncherjee Sorabjee ; Mr. M. A. Misquita ; Mr. Hormusjee Bazonjee ; Mr. Moreshwar Junardhun ; and Mr. Atmaram Pandooruug, the Secretary.

The proceedings of the last meeting were read and confirmed.

The monthly returns from the J. J. Hospital Male and Female Dispensaries for March, April, May, and June ; from the Hyperga Dispensary, for April ; and from the Bandora and the Meetheebaee Hormusjee Dispensaries, for April, May, and June last, were laid on the table ; so was also the meteorological register for the month of May last, taken at the Khandalla Charitable Dispensary, and forwarded by the President of the Society and now Acting Superintending Surgeon, Dr. C. Morehead, for the use of the Society.

With reference to the meteorological registers in general, Dr. Haines tried to impress upon the meeting that they are useful only when very accurately kept ; and that it is of the utmost importance, to enable one to take minute observations, that he should accustom himself to the reading of the meteorological instruments correctly.

It was proposed by Dr. Haines, and seconded by Mr. Gomes :— That the new Graduates, Messrs. Cursetjee Framjee, Bazunjee Rustomjee, and Cowasjee Nowrojee, be elected members of the Society.

The following books were presented to the Society :—The Annual Report of the Grant Medical College for the year 1856-57, by the Acting Principal of the Grant Medical College ; and Reports on Cholera in the Meerut, Rohilcund, and Ajmere Divisions in the year 1856, by the Medical Board.

Notes on three surgical cases, viz. 1. Penetrating wound of the chest, with protrusion of lung ; 2. Abortion, followed by tetanus and recovery ; 3. Dislocation between the 4th and 5th cervical vertebræ, terminated in death, with *post-mortem* examination, treated in the Civil Hospital, Combaconum, and communicated by Mr. P. S. Mooteswamy Moodely, of Madras ; were read.

Mr. Moreshwar Junardhun then read his paper on observations on cases of measles that came under his treatment during the late prevalence of the disease in Bombay. Mr. Moreshwar's observations seem to have extended from January to May last, during which period he treated eighty-five cases, of which fifteen proved fatal. After describing minutely the symptoms and the treatment pursued generally, he gave a diary of five of these cases. In proposing the best thanks of the Society to Mr. Moreshwar, Dr. Haines made a few observations on the state of the atmosphere favourable or otherwise for the spread of epidemics in general. On account of the lateness of the hour, several other communications were left unread, and the meeting dissolved.

(Signed)   S. A. de Carvalho,
Vice-President.

Atmaram Pandoorung,
Secretary.

Minutes of a Meeting of the Grant College Medical Society, held in the College Library, on Saturday, 8th August 1857, at half-past.four P. M.

PRESENT.

Mr. S. A. de Carvalho......   *Vice-President, in the Chair.*
Dr. R. Haines ....   *Vice-President.*

Members.

Dr. H. Giraud; Dr. Rustomjee Byramjee.; Mr. J. C. Lisboa; Mr. Bhawoo Dajee; Mr. Muncherjee Sorabjee; Mr. Ardaseer Jamsetjee; Mr. Moreshwar Junardhun; and Mr. Atmaram Pandoorung, the Secretary.

The proceedings of the last Meeting were read and confirmed. The following books were presented by the Medical Board for the use of the Society, viz. :—

1. Report of the Medical Council relative to the Cholera Epidemic of 1854.

2. Report from Dr. Sutherland, on Epidemic Cholera in the Metropolis in 1854.

. 3. Report on the Results of the different Methods of Treatment pursued in Epidemic Cholera, &c.

. 4. Report on the Results of the different Methods of Treatment pursued in Epidemic Cholera in the Provinces throughout England and Scotland in 1854.

5. Report of the Medical Council in relation to the Cholera Epidemic of 1854.

Messrs. Cursetjee Framjee, Bazunjee Rustomjee, and Cowasjee Nowrojee were then duly elected members of the Society.

The monthly returns from the Bandora, the Meetheebaee Hormusjee, and the Malligaum Charitable Dispensaries for July last, were read and laid on the table. An interesting account of the working of the Kurrachee Dispensary, for February, March, April, May, and June last, in three separate papers, by Mr. Anunta Chundroba; as well as an account of the working of the Poona Charitable Dispensary, for April, May, and June last, by Mr. Balcrustna Chintoba, were then read.

A minute account of two cases of ovarian tumours successfully treated by extirpation at the Civil Hospital, Combaconum, communicated by Mr. P. S. Mooteswamy Moodely, of Madras; and an account of a case of asphyxia from drowning, successfully treated by artificial respiration by the same gentleman, were read with much interest.

Then was read the paper of the day, giving an account of a case of diabetes, and one of retention of the placenta, by Mr. Shamrow Narayen.

After according the best thanks of the Society to the Medical Board for the present of books, and to Mr. Anunta Chundroba, Mr. Balcrustna Chintoba, Mr. P. S. Mooteswamy Moodely, and Mr. Shamrow Narrayen, for their interesting communications, the meeting was dissolved.

(Signed) R. HAINES,

Vice-President.

ATMARAM PANDOORUNG,

Secretary.

Minutes of a Meeting of the Grant College Medical Society, held in the College Library, on Saturday, 12th September 1857, at half-past four P. M.

PRESENT.

Dr. R. Haines .... *Vice-President, in the Chair.*

Members.

Dr. H. Giraud; Mr. Bhawoo Dajee; Mr. Narayen Dajee; Mr. Bajunjee Rustomjee; Mr. Cursetjee Framjee; and Mr. Atmaram Pandoorung, the Secretary. Visitor, Dr. Lownds.

The monthly returns from the J. J. Hospital Male and Female Dispensaries for July and August last, from the Bandora, the Meetheebaee Hormusjee, and the Malligaum Dispensaries for August last, were submitted, and a short account of the working of the Poona Charitable Dispensary for July and August last was read.

A full account of the Kaira Civil Hospital and Dispensary, and of the Jail and Police Hospitals for the months of April and May last, communicated to the Society by Mr. Burjorjee Ardeseer, was read with much interest.

The Secretary stated that information had been received from Mr. Ruttonjee Hormusjee, from Aden, to the effect that the paper which it was his turn to present to the Society at this present Meeting, being incomplete when the last mail left Aden, will be forwarded by the next; the subject of the paper being the medico-topographical account of Aden.

3. After according the best thanks to Mr. Burjorjee Arde-seer for his interesting communications, the meeting was dissolved.

(Signed)   C. Morehead,
President.
'Atmaram Pandoorung,
Secretary.

Minutes of a Meeting of the Grant College Medical Society, held in the College Library, on Saturday, 10th October 1857, at half-past four P. M.

PRESENT.

Dr. C. Morehead................ *President.*
Dr. R. Haines .... } *Vice-Presidents.*
Mr. S. A. de Carvalho ....

Members.

Dr. H. Giraud; Mr. P. F. Gomes; Mr. J. C. Lisboa; Mr. Narayen Dajee; Mr. Dossabhoy Bazonjee; Mr. Hormusjee Bazonjee; Mr. Moreshwur Junardhun; Mr. M. A. Misquita; and Mr. Atmaram Pandoorung, the Secretary.

The proceedings of the last Meeting were read and confirmed.

The monthly returns from the J. J. Hospital Male and Female Dispensaries, from the Bandora, the Meetheebaee Hor-·musjee, the Fort Gratuitous, the Malligaum, the Poona, and the Kurrachee Dispensaries, were laid on the table.

13

Mr. Ruttonjee Hormusjee, in a letter, expressed himself very
sorry for having been unable to forward his paper, but promised
to do so at the next meeting of the Society.

Mr. M. A. Misquita read his paper on the prevalence of fever
in Salsette, as observed at the Bandora Charitable Dispensary.
The period of his remarks extended five years and a half,' from
just the commencement of the Dispensary to the middle of the
current year ; during which 4,981 cases of fever, a little more
than one-fourth of the total admission, were under treatment,
under three classes,—intermittent, remittent, and eruptive, with
their respective numbers of 4,527, 368, and 6. He remarked,
the quotidian form, the most prevalent, next the tertian, and
least the quartan, and found persons of from twenty to forty
years of age to be most liable to both intermittent and remittent
fevers. The complications he observed of the former were
bronchitis, catarrh, diarrhœa, dropsical affections, enlarged
spleen, dysentery, hepatitis, jaundice, asthma, gastric irritation,
and rheumatism, noted in the order of their frequency ; and of
the latter, bronchitis, typhoid symptoms, hepatitis, diarrhœa,
gastric irritation, pneumonia, jaundice, dysentery, and pleuritis.'
The causes of both he believed to be the drying up, after the fall
of rain, of stagnant pools of water, of submerged jungly and un-
cultivated tracts of land, and the peculiar nature of the soil, which
absorbs moisture, and from which evaporations can take place but
slowly. He refutes the idea of salt marshes being the cause of
fevers, which prevail least in villages within or bordering on these
marshes. He remarked the intermittent and remittent fevers to
prevail most in November and least in July, commencing to
increase soon after the rains in August in almost a regular
gradation to November, and to decrease also almost gradually
from December to July. As regards treatment, he believed
quinine to be most successful, next arsenic, then cinchona, and
last chyrreta. . The paucity of cases of eruptive fever, of which
only six had been under treatment, he attributed to strong preju-
dice on the part of the inhabitants to such cases being brought
under medical treatment, and not to any want of prevalence of
eruptive diseases in Salsette.

Mr. Misquita also read an account of "two cases of worms in the nose," and remarked they were the only cases he had seen in all his practice; and concluded by reading an account of similar cases given in the fifth volume of the Indian Annals of Medical Science, by Sub-Assistant Surgeon Taruck Chunder of Allyghur.

A short discussion then ensued; and Mr. Misquita was requested to extend his observations in a future communication on the question that arose, viz. whether the maggots were produced in discharges of foul ulcers within the nose, or were independent of any ulceration whatsoever.

Then were read notes on a case of cancerous breast, communicated by Mr. Burjorjee Ardeseer. The diseased breast was successfully extirpated by him. He felt the want of the microscope in making correct diagnoses, and made a suggestion that, being as necessary as the stethoscope or the probe for the diagnosis of diseases, it may be added to the instruments of every dispensary or medical establishment.

Mr. Bhawoo Dajee being absent, no paper "on the native remedies used in the treatment of poisoning by venomous serpents" was read.

After voting the best thanks of the Society to Messrs. Misquita and Burjorjee Ardeseer, the meeting was dissolved.

(Signed)   C. MOREHEAD,
President.
ATMARAM PANDOORUNG,
Secretary.

Minutes of a Meeting of the Grant College Medical Society, held in the College Library, on Saturday, 14th November 1857, at half-past four P. M.

PRESENT.

Dr. C. MOREHEAD .... *President.*

Members.

Dr. H. Giraud; Mr. J. C. Lisboa; Mr. Bhawoo Dajee; Mr. Sudashew Hemraj; and Mr. Atmaram Pandoorung, the Secretary.

The proceedings of the last meeting were read and confirmed.

The monthly returns from the J. J. Hospital Male and Female Dispensaries, from the Bandora, the Meetheebaee Hormusjee, the Fort Gratuitous, the Malligaum and the Poona Charitable Dispensaries, were laid on the table.

Mr. Bhawoo Dajee then read his paper, " on the native remedies used in the treatment of poisoning by venomous serpents." He stated, opportunities for the study of serpents and the action of their poison are great in this country, the mortality from snake-bites being in Sind and Rutnagherry about 500 a year; that therefore the remedies employed by the natives demand a fair trial before rejecting them. He is aware that several of the believed specifics owe their reputation to want of knowledge to discriminate between the poisonous and the harmless serpents, as well as of certain seasons and circumstances of the bites, whenever the bites of venomous serpents are not fatal. He mentioned a variety of poisonous serpents of this country, and described symptoms as bearing two distinct periods of excitement and depression. The plants that have acquired greatest reputation belong, according to him, to the families of asclependeæ and aristolocheæ, and are chiefly ophioxylon serpentinum, (nágul coodú); calotropis gigantea (rooi); plumerea acuminata (pándharú chápú); aristolochia Indica; arum colocasia; tenhosanthus palmata, and sapindus emarginatus. They act by producing vomiting and purging; and when they do so, cases are believed to be safe: otherwise hopeless. He stated, the natives are aware of the use of a tight ligature above the seat of the bite, and of removing blood from it by incisions and cupping: and concluded by saying that the medicinal plants mentioned above should be employed during the stage of excitement, and ammonia, and other stimulants during depression. As the hour drew nigh, no other business was conducted; but, after a vote of thanks being given to Mr. Bhawoo Dajee for his interesting communication, the meeting was adjourned to Saturday, the 12th December 1857.

(Signed) C. MOREHEAD,
President.
ATMARAM PANDOORUNG,
Secretary.

Minutes of a Meeting of the Grant College Medical Society, held in the College Library, on Saturday, 12th December 1857, at half-past four o'clock P. M.

PRESENT.

Dr. C. Morehead .... President.

Mr. S. A. de Carvalho .... Vice-President.

Members.

Mr. J. C. Lisboa; Mr. P. F. Gomes ; Mr. Muncherjee Sorabjee ; Mr. M. A. Misquita ; Mr. Moreshwur Junardhun ; Mr. Cursetjée Framjee ; and Mr. Atmaram Pandoorung, the Secretary.

The proceedings of the last meeting were read and confirmed. The monthly return from the J. J. Hospital Male and Female Dispensaries ; from the Bandora, the Meetheebaee Hormusjee, and the Malligaum Charitable Dispensaries for November last, were laid on the table ; and an account of the working of the Kurrachee Charitable Dispensary for October last was read.

The following books were presented to the Society by the Director General, viz. :—

Hyderabad Medical Journal, vol. v.   2 copies.

ditto   ditto, vol. vi.   2 copies.

Dr. Jeannieret, on Epidemic Cholera, Diarrhœa, and Dysentery.

Mr. Rustomjee Merwanjee's paper, "on the medical topography of Panwell, and the half-yearly report of the Panwell Charitable Dispensary," was read. After mentioning the derivation of the word Panwell, Mr. Rustomjee described its situation, commercial importance, construction of its roads, footpaths, and houses ; its drainage and water-supply ; then gave a short account of the salt works, its commerce, and occupation of its inhabitants ; and concluded by suggesting to improve the salubrity of the town, by watering the roads and by increase of plantations.

The half-yearly report extends to the first six months of the current year, during which there were treated 1,422 as out-patients, and 32 as in-patients, with average daily attendance varying from 23 to 44. After a short account of different classes of diseases, the paper concluded by a list of surgical operations, meteorological tables, return of ten children vaccinated, table of admissions, and return of diseases. As there was no time left to proceed with the rest of the business, the meeting was proposed by the President to stand adjourned till Saturday next, 19th instant; and the proposition was accordingly duly carried.

(Signed)   C. MOREHEAD,
President.
ATMARAM PANDOORUNG,
Secretary.

Minutes of an adjourned Meeting of the Grant College Medical Society, held in the College Library, on Saturday, 19th December 1857, at half-past four P. M.

PRESENT.

Dr. C. Morehead............ *President.*

Mr. S. A. de Carvalho........ *Vice-President.*

Members.

Dr. H. Giraud; Mr. J. C. Lisboa; Mr. P. F. Gomes; Mr. M. A. Misquita; Mr. Moreshwar Junardhun; Mr. Cursetjee Framjee; and Mr. Atmaram Pandoorung, the Secretary.

Mr. Ruttonjee Hormusjee's paper on "medico-topographical account of Aden," in two parts, was read. It was accompanied by a plan of Aden. The first part, after a description of the situation, the ranges of hills, and the divisions of Aden, viz. the town, the isthmus, the Malla Bunder, and the Steamer Point, with a minute account of the barracks, lines, and hospitals for European and Native soldiers, officers' bungalows, quarters of Political Residents, merchants and other inhabitants, the civil and military bazars, the arsenal, the jail, the bigary lines, the Sanitarium for military and naval officers, &c. contained therein; gave an account of the inhabitants, the Arabs, Somalis, Jews,

&c., and after alluding to the soil, the food, and vegetables obtained, the supply of water, sweet and brackish, it concluded by an account of the hot and cold as the only seasons observed, the prevailing winds, and the commerce of Aden.

The second part was strictly medical. It contained an account of the prevailing diseases observed by him during two and a half years, ending in September 1857; viz. intermittent and remittent fevers, pneumonia, bronchitis, dysentery, diarrhœa, rheumatic affections, and scurvy. The subject of Aden, or Yeman, ulcer was then fully discussed. His views on this, as well as on the typhoid remittent fever prevailing epidemically during the period of observation, have been already before the Society; and after discussing the question of amputation for Aden ulcer, and the subject of transmission of those affected with it, he made an allusion to the climate of Aden, in no way peculiarly unhealthy or favourable to the production of ulcer; and then concluded by giving a suggestion for the supply of sweet water and cultivation of vegetables, and by tables of sick and unfit sent to India, and of diseases observed by him at the Military Native General Hospital during two and a half years above mentioned.

After a vote of thanks being accorded to Mr. Ruttonjee Hormusjee for his interesting communication, the meeting was dissolved.

(Signed) C. MOREHEAD,

President.

ATMARAM PANDOORUNG,

Secretary.

Minutes of the Annual Meeting of the Grant College Medical Society, held in the College Library, on Saturday, 16th January 1858, at half-past four P. M.

PRESENT.

Dr. C. Morehead . . . . *President.*
Mr. S. A. de Carvalho . . . . . . *Vice-President.*

Members.

Dr. H. Giraud ; Dr. G. R. Ballingall ; Mr. R. D. Peele ; Mr. J. C. Lisboa; Mr. Bhawoo Dajee ; Mr. P. F. Gomes; Mr. Narayen Dajee; Mr. Shamrow Narayen; Mr. Dossabhoy Bazonjee; Mr. M. A. Misquita ; Mr. Balcristna Succaram, and Mr. Atmaram Pandoorung, the Secretary. Dr. Lownds, visitor.

The proceedings of the last Meeting were read and confirmed.

The monthly returns from the J. · J. Hospital Male and Female Dispensaries, and from the Meetheebaee Hormusjee Charitable Dispensary for December, and from the Fort Gratuitous Dispensary for November last, were. laid on the table.

It was proposed by the Secretary, and seconded by Mr. Dossabhoy Bazonjee, that Dr. Lownds and Dr. Birdwood be elected members of the Society.

A retrospective address was delivered by Dr. Morehead. It contained a substantial account of the view he took of the whole of the proceedings of the Society for the year just, ended ; the attendance of the members ; the number and character of the Dispensary returns ; the nature, &c. of the papers read or communicated ; the transactions of the book club ; the cause of the failure of the Vaccination Committee ; the Society's Library, &c. A vote of thanks was unanimously accorded to Dr. Morehead for his most valuable address.

Proposed by Mr. Bhawoo Dajee, seconded by Mr. Carvalho, and carried :—

" That, in order that Dr. Morehead's views might be more generally known, the address be printed and circulated amongst the members of the Society."

A vote of thanks was also accorded, after being proposed by Dr. Giraud and seconded by Dr. Ballingall, to the Secretary, for the manner in which he transacted the business of the Society.

The annual statement of the receipts and disbursements was then

submitted, after which the election of new office-bearers for the
ensuing year took place.

It was as follows :—

Dr. G. R. Ballingall............. *President.*

Dr. H. Giraud................. } *Vice-Presidents.*
Mr. Bhawoo Dajee.............

Committee of Management.

Messrs. S: A. de Carvalho, J. C. Lisboa, and Narayen Dajee ;
and Mr. Atmaram Pandoorung, Secretary.

     (Signed) G. R. BALLINGALL,
          President.

       ATMARAM PANDOORUNG,
          Secretary.

Minutes of a Meeting of the Grant College Medical Society, held
in the College Library, on Saturday, 13th February 1858, at
half-past four P. M.

      PRESENT.

Dr. G. R. Ballingall .... *President.*

      Members.

Mr. J. C. Lisboa; Mr. M. A. Musquita; Mr. Cursetjee Framjee; Mr. Moreshwur Junardhun ; Mr. Shamrow Narayen ; Mr.
S. A. de Carvalho ; Mr. Muncherjee Sorabjee ; and Mr. Atmaram Pandoorung, the Secretary.

The proceedings of the last meeting were read and confirmed.

The monthly returns from the Fort Gratuitous and Bandora
Dispensaries for December and January last, and from the Mee-
theebaee Hormusjee and the Poona Charitable Dispensaries for
January last, were laid on the table.

Dr. Lownds and Dr. Birdwood were then duly elected members of the Society.

14

The Secretary then read an account of "a case of typhoid fever, in which the application of blister to the nuchæ was followed by mortification of the genital organs ;" and of " a case of pleuritis commencing with somewhat obscure symptoms." The points of interest in connection with the cases submitted for consideration were, whether, in the first case, the mortification was the effect of the poisonous quality of cantharides introduced into the system through the application of the blister, or was in consequence of the fever poison working upon a. constitution already predisposed to it; and, in the second, the inflammation was believed to be specific, and malaria formed the most important part, by influencing not so much the· vascular as the nervous element of the disease. After a short discussion, and after a vote of 'thanks being accorded to the Secretary, the meeting was dissolved.

(Signed) G. R. BALLINGALL,
President.
ATMARAM PANDOORUNG,
Secretary.

Minutes of a Meeting of the Grant College Medical Society, held in the College Library on Saturday, 13th March 1858, at half-past four P. M.

PRESENT.

Dr. G. R. Ballingall................. *President.*

Members.

Dr. Birdwood; Mr. J. C. Lisboa ; Mr. M. A. Musquita; Mr. S. A. de Carvalho ; Mr. Cursetjee Framjee ; Mr. Moresh-wur Junardhun; Mr. Shamrow Narayen ; and Mr. Atmaram Pandoorung, the Secretary.

The proceedings of the last meeting were read and confirmed· The monthly returns from the J. J. Hospital Male and Female Dispensaries for January and February ; from the Bandorª and the Meetheebaee Hormusjee Charitable Dispensaries for February last, were laid on the table. Mr. Lisboa read a paper, in three parts. Part first contained an account of three cases of lithotomy ; they were Parsees of 55, 3½, and 7½ years of age. The operation was successful in all, requiring 24 days in the first two, and 34 days in the last. In the first case the presence of hœmorrhoids with prolapsus ani obscured the diagnosis, and the importance of the sound with a short curve in detecting a calculus when small, and when there is an enlarged prostate, was distinctly pointed out. In the last case there was little hœmorrhage on the twelfth day of the operation, following the passage of urine for the first time through the urethra. The second part contained an account of a small calculus situated at first at the neck of the bladder, and thereby simulating symptoms of the stricture of the urethra, and then lodged at the urethral orifice, from which it was removed by slightly slitting it open. Part third contained two cases of fever, with stricture of the urethra. The fever was distinctly intermittent in type, coming on at first at regular intervals, and afterwards became irregular in both. Every mode of treatment failed in both, until the dilatation of the stricture and the administration of quinine internally, tried at the same time. The fever in one was of seven years' standing, and in the other three months'. The symptoms of stricture preceded the fever in both. After a short discussion as regards the character of the fever, and after a vote of thanks being accorded to Mr. Lisboa for his interesting communication, the meeting was dissolved.

(Signed) BHAWOO DAJEE,
Vice-President in the Chair.

ATMARAM PANDOORUNG,
Secretary.

(True copy)

ATMARAM PANDOORUNG,
Secretary.

APPENDIX BB.

ACCOUNT OF THE ANDERSON, CARNAC, FARISH, AND
REID SCHOLARSHIP FUNDS ; THE OBSTETRIC
INSTITUTION FUND; SIR JAMSETJEE JEJEE-
BHOY MEDICAL BOOK FUND ; SIR JAMSETJEE
JEJEEBHOY MEDICAL PRIZE FUND; McLENNAN
SCHOLARSHIP FUND; SIR JAMSETJEE JEJEE-
BHOY GOLD MEDAL FUND ; AND HEMABHOY
VUKUTCHUND MEDAL FUND.

Anderson Scholarship.

Dr.

1856		Amount.	Days.	Interest.
		Rs. a. p.		Rs. a. p.
May 3rd	To Cash paid to the Acting Principal Grant Medical College on this account	92 8 0	363	1 15 0
July 3rd	Ditto ditto	150 0 0	302	7 7 1
Aug. 2nd	Ditto ditto	60 0 0	272	2 10 11
Sept. 2nd	Ditto ditto	60 0 0	241	2 6 0
Oct. 3rd	Ditto ditto	60 0 0	210	2 2
Nov. 3rd	Ditto ditto	60 0 0	179	1 12 3
Dec. 1st	Ditto ditto	60 0 0	151	1 7 10
1857.				
Jan. 3rd	Ditto ditto	60 0 0	118	1 2 8
Feb. 3rd	Ditto ditto	60 0 0	87	0 13 9
Mar. 4th	Ditto ditto	60 0 0	58	0 9 2
Apr. 1st	Ditto ditto	60 0 0	30	0 4 9
,, 30th	To Balance	722 8 0 / 12,739 14 1		22 10 7 / 740 10 3
	Rupees	13,462 6 1		763 4 10

Cr.

1856		Amount.	Days.	Interest.
		Rs. a. p.		Rs. a. p.
May 1st	By Balance	12,721 11 10	365	763 4 10
1857				
Apr. 30th	By Difference of Interest at 6 per cent.	740 10 3		
	Rupees	13,462 6 1		763 4 10

Carnac Scholarship.

Dr.

1856.		Amount. Rs. a. p.	Days.	Interest. Rs. a. p.
May 3rd	To Cash paid to the Acting Principal Grant Medical College on this account	25 0 0	963	1 7 10
July 3rd	Ditto ditto	123 0 0	302	6 3 4
Aug. 2nd	Ditto ditto	50 0 0	272	2 3 9
Sept. 2nd	Ditto ditto	50 0 0	241	1 15 8
Oct. 3rd	Ditto ditto	50 0 0	210	1 11 8
Nov. 3rd	Ditto ditto	50 0 0	179	1 7 7
Dec. 1st	Ditto ditto	50 0 0	151	1 3 11
1857.				
Jan. 3rd	Ditto ditto	50 0 0	118	0 15 6
Feb. 3rd	Ditto ditto	50 0 0	87	0 11 8
Mar. 4th	Ditto ditto	50 0 0	58	0 7 8
Apr. 1st	Ditto ditto	50 0 0	30	0 3 11
		600 0 6		18 12 4
		11,801 8 3		684 4 2
,, 30th	To Balance			703 0 6
	Rupees	12,401 8 3		703 0 6

Cr.

1856.		Amount. Rs. a. p.	Days.	Interest. Rs. a. p.
May 1st	By Balance	11,717 4 1	365	703 0 6
1857.				
Apr. 30th	By Difference of Interest at 6 per cent.	684 4 2		
	Rupees	12,401 8 3		703 0 6

Dr.

Farish Scholarship.

Cr.

	Amount.	Days.	Interest.
1856.	*Rs. a. p.*		*Rs. a. p.*
May 3rd To Cash paid to the Acting Principal Grant Medical College on this account	15 0 0	363	0 14 4
July 3rd Ditto ditto	75 0 0	302	3 11 7
Aug. 2nd Ditto ditto	30 0 0	273	1 5 5
Sept. 2nd Ditto ditto	30 0 0	241	1 3 0
Oct. 3rd Ditto ditto	30 0 0	210	1 0 7
Nov. 3rd Ditto ditto	30 0 0	179	0 14 1
Dec. 1st Ditto ditto	30 0 0	151	0 11 11
1857.			
Jan. 3rd Ditto ditto	30 0 0	118	0 9 4
Feb. 3rd Ditto ditto	30 0 0	87	0 6 10
Mar. 4th Ditto ditto	30 0 0	58	0 4 7
Apr. 1st Ditto ditto	30 0 0	30	0 2 4
„ 30th To Balance	300 0 0		11 4 0
	14,000 6 4		853 2 11
Rupees	15,280 6 4		864 6 11

	Amount.	Days.	Interest.
1856.	*Rs. a. p.*		*Rs. a. p.*
May 1st By Balance	14,407 3 5	365	864 6 11
1857.			
Apr. 30th By Difference of Interest at 6 per cent.	863 2 11		
Rupees	15,280 6 4		864 6 11

Dr. Reid Scholarship. *Cr.*

1856.		Amount Rs. a. p.	Days.	Interest Rs. a. p.
May 3rd	To cash paid to the Acting Principal Grant Medical College on this account	10 0 0	363	0 7 11
July 3rd	Ditto ditto	50 0 0	302	2 1 1
Aug. 2nd	Ditto ditto	20 0 0	272	0 11 11
Sept. 2nd	Ditto ditto	20 0 0	241	0 10 7
Oct. 3rd	Ditto ditto	20 0 0	210	0 9 2
Nov. 3rd	Ditto ditto	20 0 0	179	0 7 10
,, 25th	Ditto ditto	294 5 10	157	6 5 3
Dec. 1st	Ditto ditto	20 0 0	151	0 6 7
,, 2nd	Ditto ditto	4 8 0	150	0 1 5
1857.				
Jan. 3rd	Ditto ditto	20 0 0	118	0 5 2
Apr. 30th	To Balance	478 11 10		12 2 11
		9,583 10 4		467 8 11
	Rupees	10,062 6 2		479 11 10

1856.		Amount Rs. a. p.	Days.	Interest.
May 1st	By Balance	9,594 13 3	365	470 11 10
1857.				
Apr. 30th	By Difference of Interest at 5 per cent.	467 8 11		
	Rupees	10,062 6 2		479 11 10

15

Obstetric Institution.

Dr.

1856.		Amount. Rs. a. p.	Days.	Interest. Rs. a. p.
Dec. 18th	To Cash paid	2,000 0 0	139	30 7 6
1857.				
Jan. 3rd	Ditto ditto	40 0 0	118	0 8 3
Feb. 2nd	Ditto ditto	40 0 0	88	0 6 1
Mar. 2nd	Ditto ditto	40 0 0	60	0 4 2
Apr. 1st	Ditto ditto	40 0 0	30	0 2 1
,, 30th	To Balance	2,160 0 0		31 12 1
		13,150 8 0		558 5 3
	Rupees	15,310 8 0		590 1 4

Cr.

1856.		Amount. Rs. a. p.	Days.	Interest. Rs. a. p.
May 1st	By Balance	14,752 2 9	365	590 1 4
1857.				
Apr. 30th	By Difference of Interest at 4 per cent.	558 5 3		
	Rupees	15,310 8 0		590 1 4

Sir Jamsetjee Jejeebhoy Medical Book Fund.

Dr.   **Cr.**

Date		Amount. Rs. a. p.	Days.	Interest. Rs. a. p.
1856.				
Sept. 16th	To Cash paid to the Acting Principal Grant Medical College on this account..	425 3 4	227	13 3 6
Oct. 10th	Ditto ditto	52 8 0	203	1 7 4
		477 11 4		14 10 10
1857.				
Apr. 30th	To Balance	11,025 2 3		533 12 5
	Rupees	11,502 13 7		548 7 3

Date		Amount. Rs. a. p.	Days.	Interest. Rs. a. p.
1856.				
May 1st	By Balance	10,969 1 2	365	548 7 3
1857.				
Apr. 30th	By Difference of Interest at 5 per cent.	533 12 5		
	Rupees	11,502 13 7		548 7 3

Sir Jamsetjee Jejeebhoy Medical Prize Fund.

Dr.

Date		Amount.	Days.	Interest.
1856.		*Rs. a. p.*		*Rs. a. p.*
June 3rd	To Cash paid to the Acting Principal Grant Medical College on this account......	250 0 0	332	11 5 11
Nov.25th	Ditto ditto	204 5 10	157	6 5 3
Dec. 2nd	Ditto ditto	4 6 0	150	0 1 5
		548 11 10		17 12 7
1857.				
Apr. 30th	To Balance	5,206 2 5		257 1 7
	Rupees	5,754 14 3		274 14 2

Cr.

Date		Amount.	Days.	Interest.
1856.		*Rs. a. p.*		*Rs. a. p.*
May 1st	By Balance	5,407 12 8	365	274 14 2
1857.				
Apr. 30th	By Difference of Interest at 5 per cent.	257 1 7		
	Rupees	5,754 14 3		274 14 2

McLennan Scholarship Fund.

Dr.

1856.	Amount. Rs. a. p.
April 30th. To Balance...........	7,147 9 2
Rupees	7,147 9 2

Cr.

1857.	Amount. Rs. a. p.	Days.	Interest. Rs. a. p.
Apr. 30th. By Amount received from C. J. Erskine, Esq., Surg. H. Leith, and Lt. Col. J. Swanson.	7,146 9 7		
,, ,, By Interest at 5 per cent.	0 15 7	1	0 15 7
Rupees	7,147 9 2		0 15 7

Sir Jamsetjee Jejeebhoy Gold Medal Fund.

Dr.

1857.		Amount.	
		Rs.	a. p.
April 30th	To Balance....................	3,024	3 11
	Rupees	3,024	3 11

Cr.

1857.		Amount.		Days.	Interest.	
		Rs.	a. p.		Rs.	a. p.
Mar. 3rd	By Amount received from Sir Jamsetjee Jejeebhoy, Knight........	3,000	0 0			
Apr. 30th	By Interest at 5 per cent.	24	3 11	59	24	3 11
	Rupees	3,024	3 11		24	3 11

Dr.   *The Hemabhoy Vukutchund Medal Fund.*   *Cr.*

		Amount.				Amount.
1857.		*Rs. a. p.*	**1856.**			*Rs. a. p.*
April 30th	To Balance	1,872 0 0	May 1st	By Amount of three Government Promissory Notes, received from the Collector of Ahmedabad....		1,800 0 0
			Sept. 1st	By Amount of 6 months' Interest on ditto due on the 30th June 1856.		36 0 0
			1857.			
			Jan. 21st	By Amount of 6 months' ditto 31st December 1856		36 0 0
	Rupees	1,872 0 0			Rupees	1,872 0 0

(Errors excepted)

(Signed)   E. E. ELLIOTT, Accountant General.

Bombay, Accountant General's Office, 12th March 1858.

(True copy)

HERBERT GIRAUD,

Acting Principal, Grant Medical College.

BOMBAY:

PRINTED AT THE EDUCATION SOCIETY'S PRESS, BYCULLA.

Lightning Source UK Ltd.
Milton Keynes UK
UKHW010034110123
415109UK00004B/433

9 783375 131067